PRAISE FOR THE BLOOD TRIAD

"*Blood Triad* sweeps readers across eras and locations, infusing each of these periods with her unique vampiric lore. Belasco's action scenes are brisk, and her carefully-researched characters are memorable. Her vampires are so much more than the violence of their history—within their bloody hearts, they retain their humanity."

— Tara Campbell, author of *City of Dancing Gargoyles &*
TreeVolution

"This delicious series has bewitched me. Raven Belasco has built a convincing, detailed world full of violence and romance. Here is a sharp-toothed triple threat of sensuous, deeply-felt back stories. Highly recommended!"

— Patrick Califia, author of *Mortal Companion*

BY RAVEN BELASCO

THE BLOOD & ANCIENT SCROLLS SERIES

Blood Ex Libris

Blood Sine Qua Non

Blood Ad Infinitum

Blood Triad

ALSO

Adventures in Bodily Autonomy (Editor)

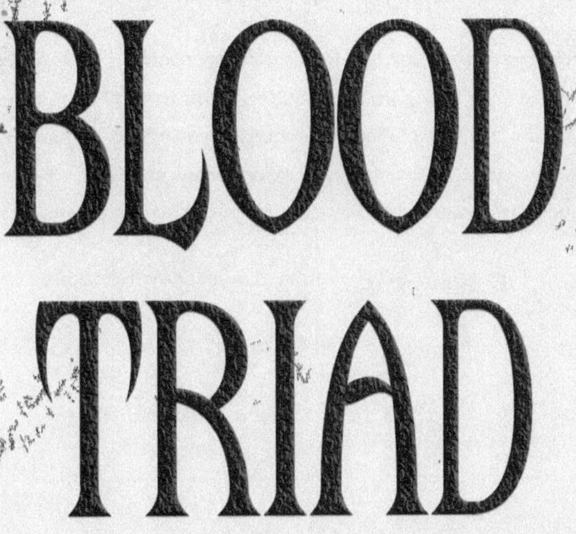

A COLLECTION
IN THE
BLOOD & ANCIENT SCROLLS SERIES

RAVEN BELASCO

Copyright © 2024 by Immoral Influence Publications

All Rights Reserved.

Library of Congress Cataloguing-in-Publication Data

Belasco, Raven.

Blood Triad / Raven Belasco

p.   cm.

ISBN: 978-1-960942-06-7

eISBN: 978-1-960942-07-4

1. Vampires—Historical Vampires—Vampire folklore—Fiction   2. Haitian History—Fiction   3. Nineteen thirties History—American 20th century—Prohibition—Fiction   4. Librarians—Fiction   5. Journeys—Journeys of personal growth—Fiction   6. American Fantasy Fiction   7. American Feminist Fiction   8. Paranormal fiction, American   9. LGBTQ fiction, American   10. Scottish History—Fiction   11. Khazars—Fiction   12. Vikings—Northmen—Fiction   13. Reproductive rights—Reproductive freedom—Abortion—Birth control—Fiction

In Memoriam Cairngorm McWomble the Terrible: *Canis meus,*

terreus et ferox, semper desiderari.

And to Archibald Alastair McWomble: You have big paw prints

to fill as my new co-editor, but as you are currently napping

beside me as I type, I think just maybe I found the right dire

terrier for the job.

"The past is never dead. It's not even past."

— William Faulkner

Contents

Author's Note on Language

This book has a bunch of words and phrases that are not in English. Some are in the am'r language, and some are in languages from around the world, since the am'r get around and often speak the language of the coun-try they grew up in, or the country they are in at the mo-ment. The am'r words are given definition when they are first used, but if you forget any of them, there is a glossary of the am'r language in the back of the book.

Likewise, there is an index of all the non-English words and phrases you will encounter along the way. If the mean-ing of those words is vital to the understanding of the sto-ry, I've made sure they get explained in the text. However, sometimes our protagonist doesn't understand what she is hearing. So you have a choice: you can experience the moment as she is experiencing it, or you can go to the index and look up the words if you don't like not knowing.

Whatever you choose, I hope you enjoy the journey!

Raven

TEETH ARE BONES

Zoraida had turned up unexpectedly. Although I should know by now to never be surprised by anything an am'r does.

"*Bonswa*, Noosh," she'd waved casually at me.

"Uh, hey, Zee," I replied with my usual aplomb, or lack thereof.

She nodded respectfully to Viv, leaning on the rails of the deck beside me, and to Nthanda, who was now the leader of all Britain. Well, not the *living humans* of the U.K., obviously. That was whomever was Prime Minster at the moment—and to be honest, I didn't know or care; I had far more important things going on—Nthanda was leader of the *British am'r*, those powerful, potentially immortal beings who were as willful and unherdable as cats, and who *really* didn't like being called "vampires."

"I have some connections that will be useful to you," she told Nthanda, and they went belowdecks to talk. Viv casually regarded the nighttime lights of the Port of London as we moved out to sea.

As did I, considering that I shouldn't be on this ship at all. My patar and gharpatar (my maker, and his maker, and so much more than the word "maker" could ever encapsulate) were going back to Sandu's underground fortress in Romania. I should have gone back *with* them, as a newly-made am'r in a dangerous world. And it was made all the more dangerous by the fact that Sandu had previously been called Vlad Țepeș—and *he* was only surpassed in enemies by his own maker Bagamil, who was the Eldest, the "Aojysht-of aojyshtaish." The most powerful people always have someone wanting to take them down, and it was no different among the am'r—indeed, it was even more so. The am'r are "more human than human," and that's not a compliment. My undeath came with built-in enemies just because of who had made me, with no consideration of who I was as my own person.

Being the newly-risen am'r descendant (the "frithaputhra," in the am'r language) of those two was my future (hopefully a very lengthy future) but I hadn't had time to ruminate on it. I'd been too busy arguing with my beloveds that I should do this Very Stupid Thing; that is, go off on my own to help hunt down Lilani, the am'r who had betrayed us. She'd directly led to my dying the mortal death and rising in my full am'r powers, forever sundering me from the kee (living human) world.

With Nthanda's help, I'd won the argument. The fact that Nthanda and his frithaputhra Viv had both promised to take care of me had definitely swayed the outcome of that dispute, but there was no point in feeling shame about that; in am'r terms, although I was stronger than when I was still living, I was an inexperienced, puny weakling. I still had that new am'r scent and factory-fresh-shine. In argument with my beloveds I had refused to admit *any* of that, insisting that my experiences before I underwent the vistarascha had made me stronger than most newly-risen am'r. Since that had indeed been their goal, they couldn't actually argue it. They didn't like me leaving their side so soon, regardless.

I had no idea why Nthanda had bothered to argue my case. It was not impossible that he just found fucking with Sandu enjoyable.

Anyway, here we were, on the MSY *Luis*, en route to Morocco. In the few days we'd been aboard, I'd seen Viv wandering around the ship, but Nthanda had closeted himself in his cabin with a laptop and phone, reaching out to connections to take us even further on our hunt. Sometimes Zoraida was with him, probably giving him that useful information. Tonight, she was sitting in the saloon with me. I was marveling that I was on this James-Bond-style yacht, in the saloon. I'd never been in a *saloon* before. (Of course, I'd never been on a Lifestyles-of-the-Rich-and-Famous kind of boat before.) It was all bright, highly-polished wood, overstuffed cushions in cream and navy nautical stripe, and gleaming brass trim. There were huge windows around the sides and back, which was no good for an am'r during the day, but gorgeous at night, particularly with this brilliant full moon lighting the ocean out to the horizon. If a kee had owned this boat, there would have been bottles of champagne in an ice bucket on the table, and plates of fancy hors d'oeuvres. Probably cigars as well. But we were am'r (except for the day crew, hand-selected kee staff who I was eager to get to know at some point on this trip, as I'd met very few kee who even knew the am'r existed, never mind worked alongside them) and so there was nothing except a mirror-polished table between us as we lounged on the sofas that stretched along the curves of the ship.

Zoraida was glowing in the moonlight, with that shining beauty that suffuses a well-fed am'r. I wondered if she had been sampling one of the day crew, something I myself was not ready to even contemplate. She seemed entirely at ease, but also felt entirely distant. I was practically sitting in this saloon by myself. She'd come in wordlessly, sat down on the other side of the long sofa, and had been looking out the window, away from me, for at least an hour now. I wondered if I never said anything, if she'd sit there in silence until sunrise, and then leave without having exchanged even one word all night.

"Zee...?" My voice was *sotto voce*, because I respected her in an almost pathetic fan-girl way and wanted to give her the excuse to ignore me if she didn't want to talk. But, of course, with am'r hearing, she could hear me above the throb of the engine, the *whoosh* and *crash* of the Atlantic waves, and the wind, which was pretty brisk at twenty-some knots.

"*Wi?*"

"I don't want to interrupt you..."

"You are not interrupting. My thoughts were old thoughts, not vital to our pursuit."

"You say, 'old thoughts.' May I ask about them?"

Zoraida laughed. It was rich and low and infectious, a sound I didn't hear often. I'd spent more time with her than most of the am'r, in our underground library in Sandu's stronghold. Zoraida was tech goddess supreme, builder of the am'r intranet, and essential supporter of me in cataloguing the am'r archives, the ostensible reason why I thoughtlessly bolted from my old life to run around like a fool with superhuman monsters, living nightly on the edge of pointless and painful death. Not that I'd gotten much chance recently to work with her in our lovely, dark, climate-controlled library cavern. Thinking of that ultimate safe space made me deeply reconsider the fuss I'd made, insisting on going off with Nthanda on his journey of vengeance. But since Zoraida had shown up for this adventure, she wouldn't have been back there with me anyway. I might as well enjoy this moment while I had it, before the inevitable violence began, when it could just be two am'r women talking in a saloon lit by patterns of moonlight reflecting off the sea.

"My old thoughts... I know you have been very curious about me—*non, non, pa enkyete!* You have been very respectful of my privacy. And I *am* very private. So, I appreciate your restraint. By not asking, you have earned the right to know me better."

I let my breath out slowly. Zoraida was right—I *had* been painfully curious about her. It was common for an am'r to take a special kind of lover, an "am'r-nafsh," that is, a "living vampire." After a ritual of exchanging blood (or "vhoon") three times, there was a transformation of body, blood, and spirit. The lovers were now connected—not just a deep soul-bond, but the am'r-nafsh blood became more nourishing to the am'r. The am'r-nafsh, while still technically alive, had become part am'r, starting to experience their strengths—and weaknesses!—before, when the mortal death came upon them, they would rest for a while in the "vistarascha" and rise again as full am'r.

It *sounds* like a great idea, to get a taste for being am'r before fully committing to it. In my experience of the past two years, it was more often frustrating and humiliating. You spent that time being neither fish nor fowl, with the *worst* of all worlds. And *completely dependent* on your am'r. I'd hated that part. It might be one reason why I was moving in the opposite direction of my patar at twenty knots an hour at this very moment.

"Thank you, Zee. I would be truly *honored* to hear anything you don't mind sharing with me." Am'r are touchy creatures; polite respect is your best policy. But I also just honestly felt that way about Zoraida. I'd made the mistake once of thinking she was "just" a talented tech geek. I'd seen only her beauty, seen only her skills for music and technology, just the very surface stuff that she'd been willing to show me. When Sandu had told me that she never made loving connections with anyone, because of past unbearable heartbreak...well, I still hadn't fully forgiven myself for such a shallow perception of her. I was quiveringly anxious to hear Zoraida's life-story now, but I *tried* to keep the overly-enthusiastic fangirl energy from showing.

She was smiling at me, and I had the rueful guess that she could sense I was like a puppy wagging my tail eagerly.

Her rare smile was wide and bright. Her lips were too full to thin out in a smile and stayed their perfect bow-shape, just slightly rosier than her skin, which was the same gorgeous ruddy brown shade as the "Smoky Topaz" Crayola crayon. (Remember that I used to work at a very small public library, please, and spent more time picking up crayons in the children's area than my degree in library science called for.) Her eyes were wide-set, almost too large to be called "almond-shaped," set off by high-arched brows. Her nose was wide and viewed from the side had an adorable little aquiline arc. She usually wore beautifully complicated braid styles, but had arrived in London with that all shaved off, revealing a perfectly-shaped head. Enough days had passed that she now had a hint of wave pattern grown in.

She glowed darkly in the moonlight, and I realized she had recently vhoon-taken, that is, drunk blood. Although if it had been vhoon-vayon, am'r love-making, I couldn't know. The ship we were on was am'r-owned and captained, but there was that day crew. It seemed like they were all available and willing to offer up their blood and bodies to the ship's am'r guests. I'd never been around this kind of fully-aware consensuality between am'r and kee before, and it made a very nice change. There truly was nothing like sharing vhoon-vayon with an am'r. For any kee crew, working on this ship had unique perks.

"*Bon*, get comfortable. It is a long story I have for you." She paused, and the smile was entirely gone from her face. I realized that it was not so much my body that I needed to get ready, but my heart.

"My story starts before me, for I have the privilege of carrying the vhoon of Kgosi"—she almost caressed the name as she spoke it: *Kho-see*—"frithaputhra of Asdrúbal, in my veins.

"Kgosi was brought over as a child in a slave ship *fout sal*. I do not know the year; the enslaved peoples had different calendars back in Africa, and then they had no calendar once they got to Saint-Domingue, only endless days of suffering and torture.

"Kgosi was sold to a French planter, renamed *Hyacinthe*"—she spoke this name with vitriolic drips of irony—"and put to the grueling work of harvesting sugar cane. I do not know how much of the history of *Ayiti* you may know, but he was at the *Bwa Kayiman*. That means in English, 'Alligator Forest.' In 1791, it was where the slaves met to plan the first rising up of the Haitian Revolution. He learned how to fight with bamboo knives and spears, while the French masters thought that their slaves were merely doing heathen dances.

"My Kgosi fought with the other heroes of the *revolisyon ayisyen*. But that first uprising in August of 1791 was just one birth pang. The colonizers did everything in their power to deny *ayisyen* their freedom. It was not until 1804 that *Ayiti* declared itself an independent nation, and France wouldn't even recognize that for years. As those thirteen brutal years ground on, an aojysht, who had been abiding in Spain in that time, heard about our struggle and decided to come and join us. He was named Asdrúbal—a Latinization of his kee name, ʿAzrubaʿal—and he was a frithaputhra of Bagamil, from whatever time in the ancient past Bagamil spent in Carthage. So you see, you and I are close cousins, *zanmi mwen*, and it is one reason your Sandu and I became such comfortable friends in these recent lonely years.

"Asdrúbal fell in love with the spirit of *Ayiti*. And he even more fell in love with Kgosi, who was at the height of his kee strength and beauty. In the midst of the bitter bloodshed, Asdrúbal made Kgosi his am'r-nafsh, and they fought side by side to liberate the island they had both come to love."

Zoraida looked thoughtful. "Now that I tell this story, this way, I realize how like Sandu's own story it is. When he was Vlad Țepeș, fighting to keep Wallachia safe from the Turks, and Bagamil fell in love with him and joined his fight. We am'r certainly prove that one can be *both* a lover and a fighter, that the combination is like..."

"Chocolate and peanut butter?" I couldn't help interjecting.

Zoraida laughed at me, but as friends laugh at each other; there was no sting. "You are still so close to being kee, *zanmi mwen*. I was going to say, vhoon and sex." She grinned, but then added pensively, "I have eaten neither chocolate nor peanut butter, you know."

Even am'r as I now was, that hit me hard. She was from such a different time than I that it was amazing we'd been able to become friends at all. I was a beloved of the oldest am'r in the world, but it had never occurred to me that he, and so many am'r walking the earth today, had never been able to enjoy a simple peanut butter cup. I'd thought that once I became fully am'r, these shocks would stop rocking my little world. Maybe in a century or five, I'd finally hit that point.

Zoraida, not terribly bothered about the lack of peanut butter cups in her life, took me back into her story. "Even after independence was declared officially recognized, *Ayiti* was extremely unstable, and it was all too easy for good men with worthy plans and goals to become corrupted by power. We got trapped in a terrible cycle of each new leader starting with promises of democratic ideals and renewal, sooner or later to become the most vile of dictators needing yet another uprising to wrest power back from them.

"Together Asdrúbal and Kgosi worked to try and rebuild as each wave of violence and misfortune hit my poor country. They helped each failed leader to be removed, and they personally saw to it that any am'r who were lured to such delicious chaos were put down before they could do too much damage."

I must have looked confused; Zoraida interrupted herself to explain. "If the only am'r who arrived on our shores had come to fight *for Ayiti*, our history would be very different. You know am'r love a battle. Think of battlefield stories and myths of the ages. Great heroes and fighters, too good to be true. Those are am'r, having fun when they can kill many kee, gorge on much vhoon, and not have other am'r come after them for adharmhem—endangering the am'r by exposure. *Bon*—as I think you know well by now—am'r do not always choose to fight on the side of *justice*. They may just choose whichever side they meet first. Or they may choose, like the *yanki*, the side which will bring them financial benefits. There were am'r among the French and British in the *revolisyon*, and then others arriving with each year of turmoil that continued.

"You could indeed class Asdrúbal among those numbers—he was there for the fight, after all. But since he came to fight on the side of freedom from slavery and oppression, and since I am the one telling this story, I count it differently. Intention does matter, and constancy as well. Asdrúbal, as a powerful am'r of Bagamil's direct vhoon-anghyaa, was not corrupted by his power. He knew what side he wished to ally himself with and he never faltered from that avocation.

"Together they fought, patar and am'r-nafsh, on behalf of those who needed protection. They had fought foreign enslavers first, and those victories were satisfying on every level, both serving their am'r need for blood and violence and their personal desire for justice. After the revolution, it too soon became clear that they must also fight against the *ayisyen* serving corrupt *ayisyen* leaders, and that was not as satisfying. It was grim work and there was no joy in victory. At least they could keep the am'r who arrived to grow fat off the disorder of those dictatorships from causing even more harm. Kgosi told me he'd lost count of how many am'r he killed when he was only an am'r-nafsh.

"In 1818, they both had such high hopes of the new president, Jean-Pierre Boyer. At this time, the Spanish colonial side of Hispaniola—this is the name of the whole island, which is today divided into Haiti and the Dominican Republic—was ready to have their own revolution to remove the colonizers. Boyer sent Haitians to remove the Spanish and unify the whole island, and Kgosi and his patar helped fight for that goal. In those early years, a taste of political stability came to Haiti, and immigrants came to build, not just invaders to take. Indeed, many Black families came from the U.S., where slavery was still legal, hoping for life in a land of true freedom and equality. It was a time of real hope, in those early years.

"But what started as stability mutated into authoritarianism and the most controlling dictator so far. To their intense dismay, they realized they had backed a control-freak tyrant. They were in the early stages of supporting the opposing liberal movement, when their fighter-and-lover partnership was sundered forever."

Zoraida paused for a moment to honor a pain that was not directly hers, but which she must have experienced strongly enough secondhand through Kgosi's recollections. She backed away from the immediate ache of it by taking time to explain to me, "In islands like *Ayiti*, which rise quickly from sea level up to high mountains, there are many caves. Some are too close to the sea and during high tide are filled with seawater, making them not useful for habitation, but many are perfect refuges for am'r. We do not have any such underground fortresses as your patar has burrowed out for himself over the centuries, but we are spoiled for choice with natural safe havens.

"However, in 1842, there was a very bad day to be in a cave. It was in the evening—not yet sunset—when an earthquake, a very big one, rocked the island and caused a tsunami as well. The cave in which Asdrúbal and Kgosi rested was utterly destroyed, burying them under not just rubble, but sheer masses of rock, a tomb in truth. Asdrúbal was deeply injured. He found his beloved Kgosi, but his kee life was ended, and the best thing to do was to leave him in the vistarascha until he was ready to rise for his fraheshteshnesh, his first meal as a full am'r. It took several days and nights, but Asdrúbal managed to pull himself up out of the ruins of the cave.

"There was an enemy am'r waiting for him. It was a rare chance, to find one of Bagamil's vhoon-anghyaa so weakened. Asdrúbal was beheaded before he could finish getting free from the deadly-tight embrace of the earth which had once protected him; after that, he was pulled free and burned down to a fine ash that blew away. An ignominious tokhmarenc for one who had lived so long, had seen the world through so many changes, and who had done so much good for those weaker and more mortal than he.

"Many months later, when Kgosi finally rose—his injuries had been very severe and it had been hard on his body to effect the transformation under such stresses—he had to experience the hunger of the fraheshteshnesh all alone. This was not very nice for the local kee population, something he always regretted. When he finally came to himself, he was full of vhoon and rage, both of which powered him through hunting down the am'r who had killed his patar—getting the story of Asdrúbal's final moments which I have just told you—and then destroying that am'r with as much deliberate cruelty as anger could warp his personality to inflict. I am glad I was not there for that, although I certainly understand it. That capacity runs in my own vhoon-anghyaa, and I am proud of it."

Zoraida looked hard at me, as though she was daring me to get offended. I felt myself almost get offended that she thought I *would* get offended, but then I remembered that I'd just been shocked about peanut butter cups a moment ago. I was still too close to being kee, it was true. "Look," I said, smiling to demonstrate my sincerity, "I've got the vhoon-anghyaa of fucking Vlad Țepeș and *I'm* proud of it." I didn't add, *That is, when I'm not curled up in fetal position, terrified that I will become a monster.*

I did add, "*You* know what I've had to do to survive these past years. How could I judge your Kgosi? And...I remember the, uh, *intensity* of the fraheshteshnesh. I needed three powerful am'r to *literally* sit on me to get me under control. Anyway, if someone actually killed Sandu or Bagamil—which they keep trying to do!—then I would never stop until I did the same thing as Kgosi. I really *get* it."

Zoraida nodded. I felt like I'd passed a little test, like she almost expected me to let her down at any point in her sharing of her story. *Not* letting her down didn't win me any points—she wasn't asking that much of me, after all—but getting it right meant she didn't stop recounting her tale. And I was desperate to hear more.

"Here is a thing I can tell you that will amuse you, Noosh. Your Dracula is not the only am'r who is accidentally famous for being a 'vampire'."

"Uh, no, Kurgan was famous, too," I replied, shuddering to remember that asshole. "He was the 'Vampire of Croglin Grange,' remember?"

"Oh, that." She waved it away without a second thought. *So much for your memory, Kurgan. I hope that* hurts, *wherever you go after the tokhmarenc.*

"*Non, non.* I mean, my Kgosi also had a story of him, told by the kee. A *yanki* named, named, oh, Uriah or Hezekiah something, the last name was D'Arcy, like something out of Jane Austen, heard of his legend—how, I know not. But he was as inspired as Byron had been, and as Stoker later was. It was printed in New York in 1819, and all the kee were scandalized by—" Zoraida paused for effect and lowered her already deep voice, "the Black Vampyre, duh duh duh!"

"Wow! Really?! I must find the original version of that for our library!"

"*Non,* you need not. It is a stupid story. It keeps no details of Kgosi's life except that he was born in Africa before coming to *Ayiti.* All else is poetic—*barely* poetic—nonsense, by an immature white man who had never been to *Ayiti* and had probably never spoken more than a few words with a Black servant or laborer in his life. It is a mostly offensive piece of trash. But the legend of my Kgosi made the shadow of an impact on the kee world, just as your Sandu has. It is not nothing."

"But, now..." She breathed in deeply, and with the out-breath came more words. "Myself, I was born in 1904, the year *Ayiti* celebrated one hundred years of independence. It was not a magic number. All I remember of my childhood is hunger and adults talking about our presidents being overthrown or killed. When I was fifteen the *maren*—that is our word for Marines—from your country invaded and occupied mine. It was a desperate time for my people. The politicians who sent their military to invade a country which was no threat to them said they were trying to bring 'stability.' But we knew that the Americans had never supported a free *Ayiti*. They wanted us to be enslaved again. They had stood by and watched as European colonizers tried again and again. Now they were ready to do it themselves.

"Two years later, everything changed. Well, not for *Ayiti*—the *okipan Ameriken* still made our lives hell—but for *me*. I was fighting with the resistance. They called us 'Cacos.' It is a bird found only on our island. Like that bird, we hid under leaves to surprise our enemy. We stayed up in the mountains, under the leaves, but when we came down upon them, we killed ten of them for each one of us. Those big, well-fed *maren Ameriken* with all their guns, they were afraid of us.

"I was seventeen. I dressed as a man because I was fighting with men, and, *bon*, we have a saying, '*dan konn mòde lang*'—'teeth are known to bite the tongue.' People who are on the same side may still hurt each other. Haitian-women are *strong*; they are fighters in our history. You can't have a revolution without women. In fighting the dictator Boyer, the one I told you about before, women of the Léogâne Arrondissement—this is south and west of Port-au-Prince—dragged two cannon from a fort, and killed at least thirty soldiers. And this is just one example. The families of the Cacos often followed them up into the mountains, so it was not *only* gangs of men. And the *fout maren* certainly took that as an excuse to execute women and children, as "auxiliaries" of the Cacos. But mostly, I did not want my gender to slow me down. I was so angry and I wanted to fight alongside the men, be treated as one of them. My face was rounder, then, more like a boy, and I was not such a pretty boy when I was covered with mud and sweat and blood.

"Kgosi was fighting with us. He was a legend among the Cacos. Of course I did not yet know his full history, the am'r part of his life. At this point he was more of a myth to me than anything else. For kee on the outside, looking in, he certainly seemed more like a story we made up to inspire ourselves than one of us. He would show up where their most brutal fighters were, and go straight for them, killing any *maren* that got in his way without pause. To us, it seemed like something out of a story.

"As with years past, there were am'r among the *yanki* as they occupied our land, coming for the joy of combat, for the free-flowing vhoon, and for even base financial gain. It was Kgosi who knew them by smell, 'esteshcinasti' in our am'r tongue. He would scent them over the kee blood, the gunpower, the sweat and voided bowels, the stench of war. He would throw himself upon them. He was, what is the word in English? A fighter crazed in battle?"

"A 'berserker'."

"*Wi*. That is what he was. I never knew him before Asdrúbal had been killed, but when I met him, his only life was revenge and killing. Hatred flowed in him instead of vhoon, hatred for those who kept trying to enslave our peoples, but more hatred for any am'r who allied themselves with the colonizers who broke like endless waves upon our island.

"It was later that he told me this, as I lay in his arms, but Kgosi had a passion that the am'r could become a force for good in the world of the kee. You know that amongst the am'r, strength and power are all, and the vile beliefs of misogyny and racism are proven to be false; the am'r who cling to them find those miscalculations fatal. Kgosi wanted to bring that to the kee; his great dream was to dispatch those racist leaders and politicians powerful in the kee world, and use am'r influence to raise up equality-minded leaders. He wanted to lift all who were in bondage, not only outright slavery, but those suffering under racist systems as well. He would see *Ayiti* raised up first, and then spend his long am'r years dedicated to erasing racialism across the globe. As you know, he did not live long enough even to help his beloved island...."

When Zoraida did not resume her story, I looked up at her. Am'r cannot cry, so there were no shining tracks down her cheeks. But the glowing good health she'd exuded earlier was dimmed. She looked drawn, like a decade of age had crashed over her, a far bigger, darker wave than the ones making the movement of the ship so extreme.

She felt my eyes on her, looked over at me. "I have never recovered from the loss of him, you know. Maybe it is in the vhoon-anghyaa from Asdrúbal, that none of his fritha-puthraish can ever recover from the loss of their patar. Or perhaps we are compelled to love only those who can meet our love at such a deep level? In any case, I understand Kgosi's heartbreak, his passion in the face of loss, for I myself have burned with it ever since I lost him....

"But this is out of order. I was telling you, my friend Noosh, about the time before I knew Kgosi except as legend. Of course I had heard his name, stories upon the lips of all Cacos. I had seen him fighting from the distance, a frenzied whirlwind of violence, but it would have never occurred to me to try and meet him. He was like a rock star for the Cacos, a celebrity of bloodshed and revenge.

"One evening there was a battle with the *maren*, maybe uglier and more brutal than usual, maybe not. We Cacos did what you would call guerrilla warfare, using the landscape we knew well against the invader's ignorance. We lured the *maren* into traps, we appeared when they least expected us and vanished when they thought they would slaughter us all. But they were so vastly better armed than we, superior in technology and sheer amount of armament. We had only pikes, machetes, old rifles. Our tactics kept us alive, and sometimes we won victories which fueled our hunger for more and demoralized their *blan* asses. But days like this one, we had as many losses to mourn as triumphs to celebrate.

"I was slumped around the fire with a few men I knew, almost too exhausted to stay awake for the gamey *kòk* that had been found and was now cooking unevenly over a spit. It was better than our usual dinner of a few bananas or breadfruit. By this point I was numb to violence, but I had lost someone I cared about that evening, in a nasty little skirmish that was nothing but a waste of ammunition and life; it had gotten neither side any good thing.

"I was ready to give up on dinner, to go away to find a private place to lie down and accept the gift of unconsciousness, when a stranger joined us around the fire. The others looked up, recognized him, and made room for him. They offered him the best part of the singed fowl, and he turned it down politely, telling the men that he had dined already. It was those gentle manners that woke me up, as well as the deference the men showed him. Both were rare enough things among the Cacos, who were rough and ready and very egalitarian.

"As the firelight played over his features, I watched him through mostly-closed eyes, pretending I was not looking at him. A strong face: broad forehead over big round eyes. A low, wide nose balancing them perfectly. Cheekbones dramatically pulling your eyes down to full lips, shaped amply for speaking strong words or pressing true kisses. His beard was untended at that time, and his hair had been unbeautifully hacked off at some point and was growing back in every direction, but most fighters looked thus. The firelight caught the warmth of his dark brown skin, like the heartwood of the bayawonn tree. Like the tree, he had extraordinary depth in his roots, and was durable and reliable, hard and heavy. Tough in body and spirit. And, like the bayawonn, he had thorns you best watch out for....

"*Ahhhh*...it still makes my heart feel like it has been pulled out, being squeezed to pulp in a tight fist, to think back upon his face, the face I loved from that moment on. *Ou se lanmou kè mwen*, Kgosi...."

The flood of her words dried up. I didn't dare interrupt her memories. I could feel the pain of her loss so strongly. I'd never yet experienced that particular loss, although in the past two years I'd come too close, too many times. She'd made her emotions fully accessible, not just to my imagination, but to my soul. I ached for her, *with* her.

"I am sorry," she said, coming back to the present, to the moonlit saloon, rising and lowering with the waves. "I said that to him many times: 'You are the love of my heart.' That has not changed, in all the years since.

"But I was speaking of that night.... He spoke to us then, commiserated with our losses, encouraged and inspired us with his words. He quoted Péralte, 'I will not stay under the domination of the whites.' When one man complained that the ancestors were no more, he argued passionately that no, our ancestors were there with us still, and they had fought off tyranny and slavery before. And with their help, we would do so again.

"His passion fired all our souls. I, who had been so jaded with every kind of exhaustion, felt my body and heart fill with fervor again. The others were drawn to him, trying to sit near him, asking him, "Kgosi, what do you think of this?" and "Kgosi, what do you think of that?" and so I understood who he was, that the myth sat across the fire from me.

"He kept a space around himself, a distance from those who fawned over him. I saw this, and I kept my own space, not wanting to make a fool of myself. I felt the same eagerness as the rest of them, and I was uncomfortable with it. Who was this stranger, that we all threw ourselves at his feet? How dare we trust myths, we whose stories always ended badly?

"After they were all asleep and snoring, I lay a little distance away, my sleep disturbed despite my exhaustion. When I closed my eyes, I saw the firelight on his face, on the muscles of his strong arms. So instead, I stared up into stars shining through the canopy of branches. I did not hear him approach, but then his dark form blotted out the interplay of light and shadow. I sat up, my machete ready in my hand.

"'*Non, non*,' he said, voice low. 'I only wish to speak with you. Do not fear me.'

"'I fear nothing,' I told him, because that is the sort of thing you say, when you are young and constantly afraid.

"'*Nan kou pa*,' he said. *Of course not.* He spoke very gently, his eyes shining at me in the starlight. 'I have heard from the others that Delivrans is a fierce fighter.'

"Dressed and living as a boy, as I said before, I had chosen that masculine name as protection.

"'So, you bring deliverance,' Kgosi said to me, taking me seriously as you do any solemn child. That is what *Delivrans* means in *Kreyòl*.

"'I do the work of the Good God and the *lwa*. You said the same thing back at the fire.'

"'I did. I believe it. But I can sense how dispirited you are, Delivrans. You are tired of trying to bring deliverance and failing over and over—*non, non*, I do not mean you are less of a fighter! I just mean, I can feel that you have been worn down by these battles that lead only to meaningless death, not victory.'

"'Is it wrong to mourn needless deaths? We fight this unfair invasion of our land. But the *blan* should not be trying to take our land and our liberty from us! This is a *stupid* war, and I hate it all.'

"'You are not wrong. But at all times, all over the world, invaders come to steal, to conquer, to colonize. They come especially to our island, for it is bountiful and beautiful. Every generation must be prepared to fight for what is theirs.'

"'And so we never move forward! We just fight and lose everyone we love. We watch everything we love burn. We fight until we are all broken. We have no time to heal before we must fight again.'

"'*Sa ki pa touye ou, li angrese ou.*' He shrugged. It made me angry.

"'What does not kill you, fattens you.'

"*Merde.* None of us is getting fat. Too many of us are dying, too. Don't throw stupid old proverbs at me, *enbesil.*"

"He smiled, still so gentle. 'You are right. This is not fair. It *is* stupid. But, for now, it is what we must do. We must defend our land and our families. The only other choice it to give in. Would you be a *kolaboratris?*'

"A *collaborator.* The word smacked my mind. Those have always been our worst enemies, those who took the side of the *blan,* and worked against their own kith and kin. Who chose comfort over freedom, money over love, security over liberty. *That,* I could never be. I would sleep in dirt and uncertainty and fight for my people. That was the only choice for me. And yet. Why did my people keep having to make this choice? With every supposed good leader of our land, we ended up with a self-declared emperor or dictator in self-denial. Each time, we faced that terrible choice again, support a villain and close our eyes and pretend we haven't sold our souls...or else fight and die, keeping our souls pure.

"'Are those our only options?' I asked him, hurting because I knew the answer already.

"'So far in our history, they have been,' he replied, the deep scars of history echoing in his tones as well. 'The white man only understands violence; we can only get him to comprehend that strong language. We keep telling him: we are not going to be good slaves, for we are not afraid of death. We will *make* him hear us if we keep saying it with blood.'

"'But. What about our own people? Why must they too only hear that strong language?'

"'Who have we been taught by, if not the *blan*? We try, with every generation, to shake off the lessons they taught us at the end of a whip. But greed, self-indulgence, avarice, meanness, megalomania, are they not all just *hunger*, in twisted forms? We have been hungry for too long. Is it no wonder that some of us do not find ourselves, like kids with a sweet dessert, eating until we are sick? Except, these are men, and they embody all of *Ayiti*, and they make all of us sick with their unquenchable appetites. We must get past starving, to be able to think about something more than our bellies.'

"How can we, when they keep us starving?"

"'You know this. *Premye so pa so*: a missed first try does not count—one must roll up one's sleeves and try again. And again, and *again*. We are a brave and willing people. We have wise minds and strong hearts in each generation. We must keep trying until we get it right. I will keep trying; this I promise you. I will never tire of this fight.'

"When he said this, I felt such a weight to his words. To my eyes, he looked in his twenties, like maybe he could have been fighting only a decade. But something deep inside me heard that he had been fighting far longer. It made no sense, but I had begun to relax in his presence, to feel a safety I had not felt since I was very small. And with relaxation, the bone-deep exhaustion began to finally overtake me.

"'Go to sleep, Delivrans. I will deliver you from evil while you rest.'

"In the morning he was gone, but I had slept well and deeply. We went maybe a week after that without seeing action. We stayed up in the mountains, tended to those who were injured, rested, sharpened our weapons. Now that I had met Kgosi, I heard his name everywhere. The men spoke of him as a Louverture or Dessalines. The women were a bit more earthy, with a sparkle in their eyes.

"We tangled with the *fout maren* wherever we could get the advantage of them. Often this was in the eye-confusing lengthening shadows of dusk, or if the *maren* made the mistake of being outside of the cities or their forts at night, we would teach them valuable lessons in how unwelcome *yanki* were in our country. They could not tell the difference between the average *ayisyen* farmer and a Caco, and they had rules to shoot anyone *suspected* of being a Caco on sight. They used *ayisyen* women only as good enough to fuck, but not treat as human, so there was not one of us who did not have at least one family member or friend to avenge. And as the years of *okipan Ameriken* went by, those numbers added up and up."

"I am sorry, Zee—I'm sorry to interrupt, but I'm even more sorry that I don't know *anything* about this. Why were the U.S. Marines even in Haiti?"

"*Pa gen bon rezon*—no good reason. They said it was because our society had broken down, and they were come to teach civilization to us savages. But in fact, they wanted our harbors for their navy ships, as well as our land for the same reason all colonizers do. And they wanted to make sure we could never choose to align with enemies of the United States; our island was 'strategic.' In 1914, the US sent *maren* the first time to come and take all the gold in our government's reserves. They *said* it was to ensure we would be able to pay off our debts, a forcible paternalism, but it was international armed robbery, and a bonus side effect was helping to destabilize *Ayiti*. They were trying to force us to *reach* for our chains. They wanted to enslave us again, this time calling it 'democracy.' A year later, having 'helped' our country to the breaking point, they helped themselves to everything else. They imposed martial law on our sovereign nation with their superior firepower, then they placed their puppet as our supposed leader. They suppressed our free press. They repressed our religion and jailed us or killed us for practicing it. They used their control of the government to get our companies to do business with American companies, at their terms. They did land grabs and moved American companies onto our soil, displacing farming families who had been one with their land since the *revolisyon*.

"They made us live in terror of their capricious violence—they were free to kill us if they didn't like how we looked at them. They were free to rape our women, for whomever tried to stand up to them was lynched as a lesson to others. They burned any village that they thought were hiding us Cacos. They bribed or threatened our people, turning them into spies against their own friends and families. They conscripted, arrested any man they wanted for the *corvée*, which was slavery in all but name, a kind of national chain gang. They said they were building schools and hospitals for us, but how can buildings built by forced labor be democracy?

"One time, for example, they came across a funeral wake, family and friends singing for the dead, and they took away all the men by force; they even took the carpenters who were building the coffin. The women they left had to just bury that poor body in the dirt.

"I remember seeing our men roped together cruelly, driven like slaves, breaking their backs to build roads so the foreign oppressors could hunt us Cacos down easier. They tortured the men in the *corvée* by setting dogs upon them, and with the *Baton-lamnò*: the baton of death.

"Many of our villagers had never seen airplanes even once in their lives—until the bombs were falling down from them. And the U.S. military did not care who they bombed.

"They came to our country and called us the slurs of your country. In *Ayiti*, '*nèg*' means 'a person'...but they called us 'niggers' and it meant we were less than people, in their eyes. It did not matter if our skin was dark as night or almost as pale as theirs. It did not matter if we had been educated in the finest universities in Europe, more polished than the eighteen-year-old high school dropouts from Georgia or Texas who were now pointing guns and throwing stones at us, or playing football with our friends and family members' decapitated heads. They called us 'shaved apes' and 'savage monkeys' or just 'animals.' They called us that so they could excuse to themselves how they killed us indiscriminately, beat us, burned us alive, and stole the humanity from those they left alive. And how could they honestly claim to want to bring democracy to us, when people with skin the shades of ours in their own country were still denied full citizenship?

"For our parts, we called the U.S. Marine Corps, *Use Sans Moindre Contrôle*, which means, 'Has No Self Control.' And many stronger terms.

"The leader of the Cacos was, for a time, Charlemagne Péralte. I mentioned him before. He was a great man, who showed by example how to fight for one's country. They hunted him up and down the island; time after time he escaped. The final time, he did not. You can see a picture they took of his dead body online if you like, the bullet holes in him, tied to a board, wearing only a cloth over his loins. He was only thirty-three. They took that picture around to show everyone in *Ayiti* that they had killed their last hope.

"And, as a wise woman from my country has pointed out, over a hundred years after the U.S. Occupation began, the *désocupation* has yet to come."

I stared at Zoraida as she rained these facts down upon me. Disgust and horror raised up in me to meet that truth. How had I not known this? I, a librarian, a *keeper of knowledge*. I'd felt I'd had a decent grasp on history, on an understanding of the world and my country's place in it. But I'd had no understanding of this. Learning it now shook me to my core. The world had changed from the one I thought I knew. I didn't feel certain of my place in it anymore.

Finding out that vampires were real was easier than this.

Zoraida watched me, face expressionless, eyes glittering in the wave-reflected moonlight.

I tried a few times to gather my thoughts into words. Each time, the rush of my reactions crashed down on me with waves far bigger than the ones bouncing our ship around. Finally, I squeaked out, "I—had no idea..."

"Few Americans do. At the time, your press reported that we were savage animals needing the order and restraint imposed from outside. That we were children—*at best*—needing mature adults to teach us how to be civilized. The government and the press told you that your military was making the world a better, safer place. Is that not what you are always told? And you always want to believe it. Since that time, few people outside *Ayiti* wish to remember what was done. America got what it wanted, stole the resources of our land, stripped us bare as the Europeans had done. You left your factories and inequitable trade deals and moved on. You come back to renew those inequities after every earthquake, every hurricane; when we are at our weakest, you swoop down again and, with paternalistic lies, you do your best to ensure that *Ayiti* will never catch up, will never get equal footing in the global economy. The kindest way to look at it is incompetence: that the money raised for humanitarian relief just *accidentally* all goes to international NGOs, and not to *Ayiti* or her people. But we who look back over history, we see the patterns repeat again and again. It is *funny* how the same accidents keep happening.

"Americans invaded us yet again in 1994. Do you remember that? This one was within your lifetime."

"I'm...so sorry." It was so inadequate, but what else could I say?

"I mostly do not bother to tell Americans these things, but I knew if I spoke that you would hear. This is why telling you my story, and the story of my country, is not a waste of my time. Do you understand now why we were fighting your U.S. Marine Corps in my country?"

"Yes. *I hate it.* But I understand it. Please, continue with your story. I want to hear all of it, please."

"My personal story is as painful to hear as is the story of my country. I will hurt to tell it, and you will hurt to hear it, but we will make the sorrow less by going through it together." She paused, and I could almost see her slipping back into the past.

"I was saying, when women spoke of Kgosi, they had a certain sparkle in their eyes. There was one afternoon when the fighters had come back to where the women and children had set up a semi-permanent village, real huts to sleep in, and real cooked food at night, fried meats and vegetable stews. It was a holiday, *Mange Loa*, where we feast the gods, whose power increase at that time. We were far up in the mountains, and felt safe to have cooking fires and music and dancing.

"I sat by *Madanm* Sanité, who was the oldest person I had ever known. She must have been over a hundred years old—or at least she looked like it—and she talked as if she had lived forever. She was still as active as anyone, gathering water and firewood herself, foraging for herbs for her medicines, dancing like a woman who had lived only twenty years.

"She had, upon seeing me, demanded that I be her personal helper that day. You do not turn down grannies such as *Madanm* Sanité. As I helped her peel plantains and mash them, we listened to the conversations around us. Kgosi had come up again, a subject oscillating through the makeshift village from one group to another. It was wondered how many years he had been a fighter before this newest invasion. Who had taught him the *Tire Machèt*—Noosh, this is *ayisyen* martial art: machete combat, at the intersection of fencing and dancing and brutal violence—that he was now teaching the young ones in the evenings when it seemed safe enough to gather. He was skilled with every gun he put hands on, the old muskets we had and the new ones we managed to steal from the *yanki*. He showed anyone who wanted to know how to aim more precisely, the best ways to care for their weapons.

"This lead, in certain groups, to jokes about how well Kgosi handled his own weapon. More than one woman claimed to have intimate knowledge of this. I must not have schooled my face well enough, for *Madanm* Sanité grinned her few remaining teeth at me and said, 'They are fools, speaking foolish words. Never mind them.'

"'He does have quite a reputation,' I muttered back to her.

"'Do you believe everything you hear? *Lang pa lanmè, men li ka neye-w.*'" Zoraida looked up from her past. "Noosh, that means, 'The tongue is not the sea, but it can drown you.'"

She looked out the window again. "I replied to her, 'If the same words are on so many lips, does that not give them weight?' The gossip was making me angry. I did not dare take it out on that honored elder, but I was more curt than I typically would have been.

"*Madanm* Sanité smirked at me. I ground my teeth, as old people often make you do. '*Souke tèt pa kase kou,*' she laughed. She knew she was driving me nuts with her wise sayings. This one meant, 'You can shake your head, but do not break your neck.'

"'Those women boast of things they *wish* were true,' she added. 'I know every man each of those tale-tellers has lain with. Not one of them can claim Kgosi's bed and have told the truth.' She kissed her teeth dismissively.

"'Kgosi, he has things he wants from a lover. He has *appetites*. But he mostly does not satisfy them with us country-folk. He goes to the cities, feeds his hungers without love.'

"I was disgusted by those words. 'So, he is just a dog? That is worse than if he had slept with everyone here who claims it!'

"'You misunderstand, *ti gason.*' *Madanm* Sanité gave me a knowing look as she called me 'boy,' and I froze. But her smile softened, and I knew my secret was safe with her. 'Kgosi is unlike any man. His needs are different. He is our protector. He cannot give our women what they want, so he does not toy with their hearts or use their bodies. They get enough of *that* from the *fout blan.*'

"'I spoke with him,' I told her. 'He did not seem different to me.' I was lying and she knew it.

"'Is there any fighter like him? Is there any man so clean, out there? I am sure you have seen him covered with blood, but does he stink with sweat, like you and I do? Has he ever amazed you with his strength or his stamina?'

"'We have all fought past our last strength…' I demurred, but she knew my obstinacy was weakening.

"'Don't be dumber than you must be, *gason*. You know what I mean.'

"I am not incurably stupid; I kept my mouth shut and let her talk. 'And, think you: when have you seen him during the day?'

"I thought back. I had seen him when the sky was lightening to a pale slate-blue before sunrise. I had seen him as dusk turned our fighting bodies into deadly shadows. I had seen him killing our enemies in the stark moonlit shades-of-grey. But never had I seen daylight on his beautiful skin.

"'You see it, *gason*. Unlike those silly girls over there. With you, *je wè, bouch pe*.' She had said of me, 'The eyes see, the mouth is shut.' I could not argue with that. And I was now more than ready to hear anything she would tell me.

"'He is another kind, one greater than us. *Non*, not a *lwa*, although who can say if they did not make him to protect us. *That* is what I believe. That they imbued him with powers. They do not need to be invited to ride him; he long ago gave up half his soul. He is their hand in this world. But he is gentle with it. He kills our enemies but does not harm those who do not deserve it. Most never see him, not truly, like those gossiping little fools over there. He is only a legend to them, even as he moves among us.'

"'How—how do you know this, *Madanm*?'

"'I just bet you want to know, *gason*!' she cackled. I waited in polite silence. I knew these old ones. They liked to test your patience; they had learned it long ago and liked to see the young ones struggle with it.

"She could not help herself with bragging now, however. 'I know because he *showed* me. What the little fools claim, I tasted, back when I was a ripe mango myself.

"'One night it was so very hot, I could not sleep. All I wanted was to go for a swim, in a hidden pool that only my village knew about. I lived far up in the *Montagnes Noires* back in those days. I snuck out and made my way so quietly along the stream until I was deep in the woods. The night was cooler under the trees away from the village, and the sounds of the stream and the birds and other night creatures was like music in the darkness.

"'I got to the pool and slipped off my dress. The water, fed from higher up in the mountains, was almost too cold. But it was worth it to slowly lower my body in, for suddenly the night was delicious, not oppressive.

"'I nearly jumped out of that pool and my skin as well, when a voice spoke softly from too close by, telling me not to be afraid.'

"Noosh, as the elder told me that, I remembered Kgosi surprising me as I rested, not too long before. It put a shiver down my spine. But I would not have interrupted *Madanm* Sanité for the world. 'A beautiful man sat by the pool. I had neither heard him arriving nor making himself comfortable. I had never seen him before, but when he told me his name, it was one I had heard in stories the men told after they had been drinking rum.

"'Well, *gason*, you do not need too many details of what happened after, but it is enough to say he loved me, loved me like none other, loved me as I have never been loved since. And as he loved me, he took my blood, his teeth worshipful in my flesh.'"

Zoraida interrupted herself again. "Noosh, you are not conversant with our Vodou, but when she told me that he drank her blood, it was not something that seemed too strange to me. For one, she had already said that the *lwa* were in him, that he was something different because of that. For two, I had grown up with rituals where blood is a sacred gift from an animal, strengthening your spirit with its own. It was in no way a novel idea to me, just a different version of the sacred and ceremonial. I kept my mouth shut and listened to all *Madanm* Sanité saw fit to tell me.

"'After that, he visited me a few more times, before I joined my husband, the old way, in *plaçage*. And I wouldn't have minded if he visited me again *after*, to tell the truth, but he was too respectful.' *Madanm* Sanité paused, caught my eye, and continued, 'That man who made love to me in the pool, he does not look a day older now than he did that night. I see him, now and then, through the years. He always has a smile and polite word for me. Heh, I wouldn't mind if he'd visit me in the night again—even as ancient as you think I am!'

"She pierced me with a knowing look, 'You want him, do you not, *gason*? I see you tense with jealousy as those fools chatter. You cannot be jealous of one such as him. The *lwa* are very draining to mortal flesh; he must require much sustaining to continue being half-man, half-god.'

"'I do *not* want him,' I told her, stiffly. 'I've only spoken to him once.'

"'That matters not,' she laughed at me with her dry old-lady cackle. 'You are already his, and too bad for you if you do not know it! But I hope you find out soon, for it is a pleasure beyond words in this harsh world. You deserve good loving. You deserve to be a *woman*—not a boy who only kills and knows nothing of love.'

"I quickly looked around us, but no one was close enough to hear her. '*Mèsi, Madanm*," I thanked her. I wanted to be angry at her words, but that was only to conceal how deeply they touched me. *Madanm* Sanité smirked and said she did not require any more of my help. I was free to escape her uncomfortable conversation.

"I was physically a part of the celebrations that day, but my mind was elsewhere entirely. I could not stop thinking about Kgosi and all I had learned about him. As we ate, drank, and danced, his face flashed through my mind. I remembered every glance I'd ever caught of him fighting fearlessly and tirelessly, the muscles of his arms and chest caught out by sunset or moonlight. When the *manbo* led the holiday service, I was as tranced as any there...but not by the chanting or ritual, but by the reflections of this 'different' man, replaying over and over in my brain.

"I drank too much rum, in consequence. At some point in the evening, I found myself sitting some distance from the celebrants, far enough that the drumming was not throbbing in my brain pushing out all thought, but just a counter-rhythm to my heart. The temporary village was in a space between trees that was barely a clearing, so finding a private area in which to sit and think did not take me too far.

"He snuck up on me again. Between one moment and the next, he was sitting beside me in the dirt. My whole body shocked to belated warning, then I forced myself to relax back against the tree trunk I'd been leaning upon.

"'I hate how you do that,' I complained, my tongue relaxed by the rum that made the night spin comfortably around me.

"'The *blan* hate it even more,' he replied dryly. 'I do not think you hate it in those circumstances.'

"'Of course not,' I admitted. 'But it is different when you use it on my enemies than when you use it on me.'

"'My deep apologies. I will make sure to stomp my feet and approach you slowly and inelegantly from now on, my little Deliverer.'

"'I will accept that,' I told him, the rum making it easy for me to smugly receive his attentions.

"We sat quietly together for a while, listening to the beat-patterns of the voices and drums. Finally, I asked him, 'Did you see *Madanm* Sanité?'

"He smiled, a sight that grabbed my heart too easily. 'She is out there dancing like an *adolesan*. She would tire *me* out!'

"'She is dancing like she is as young as when you first met her?' I asked with deliberate carelessness.

"'Yes, exactly. Same smile, too. But she has only gotten more goat-headed with time.'

"We laughed together at that, and then there was a pause. Finally, he said, 'So, I see she has told you about me. How...do you feel about what you have learned?'

"'I...am not so surprised,' I told him.

"'Do you mind it?'

"'*It* helps you fight our enemies, does it not?'

"'*Wi*. But I would like to do more with you than just fight our enemies together.'

"It was both a surprise to hear this and no surprise at all. 'Would you?' I asked him. '*Poukisa?*'

"'Why? I could joke about liking pretty boys,' he responded, with that smile that had too much power over me. 'But I would rather be serious and tell you that I admire your strength. You fight men much larger than you with no fear, and you kill them with no hesitation. But you are more than a fighter. You have heart. You are always compassionate to children and elders. You give everything of yourself to our people; you give your time and hands, and you would give your life just as straightforwardly. Not many are like you, so full of love.'

"'It does not feel like *love*. All I feel is anger. That is why I fight. That is all I can do. I will not plant a garden that will only be trampled under the foot of the *blan*, nor bring babies into this terrible world just to be abused, enslaved, and murdered. I can only kill.'

"'Oh, *chouchou*, that anger is pure love. Do you ever take that anger out on the weak? *Non*. Your anger is a force to protect those who need it. That is *love*, simple and absolute. You and me, we are the same in this way.'

"'You are...different. Much stronger than me, at the very least.'

"He shook his head, waved his hand as if to waft my argument away like a bug. 'Physical differences mean nothing. We are the same at our core with what makes us who we are. However. Those differences could be...minimized. It would only take a little loving to make you more like me, for always. If you decide you want it.'

"'A little loving.... But, a little loving did not make *Madanm* Sanité different like you.'

"'Ha! She may be *more* than me. She may outlast all of us!' But I did not laugh with him, and he answered me more seriously, 'There are ways to have either, ehhh, outcome. With *cheri* Sanité, I only took what she gladly offered me. With you, I would gladly give back to you in equal measure. If you drink of my blood a number of times, it would strengthen your spirit with mine. While you lived, you would be more than mere human—not quite as powerful as I. Then, when in natural course you die, you would awaken again to find yourself in the same physical condition as you find me.'"

Zoraida met my eye. "Well, I do not need to repeat to you, *zanmi mwen*, how the rest of that conversation went. He told me of the strengths and limits of being an am'r and an am'r-nafsh, the still-living half-am'r. He talked to me until the sun was about to rise. My head was starting to ache from too much rum and too many new thoughts.

"'Now I know you must get into darkness before the sun is up,' I told him, and made a face. 'I think I will, too, for my head is already starting to pound harder than those drums.'

"'Come with me,' he invited, 'and I will sweetly cure that hangover in a safe dark place. Choose to go down the road with me, and your first steps will make you free from pain and bring you much pleasure.'

"I could see no reason not to go with him and let him cure my hangover. I could see no reason not to let him strengthen my spirit with his, through the sharing of blood. And love. I had not known it, but I was starving for love, to counter the pain and fear and death that was so much a part of my life.

"I'd had a few graceless fumblings with boys my age; while I was not a virgin, I was not experienced in passion. And *passion* was what Kgosi taught me that night, and every night after, for after that first night, we were never separated again until his tokhmarenc, that most final of deaths, sundered our hearts forever."

Zoraida's face softened, and I was shocked at how different she looked. Even when she was at her happiest with me in the archives, humming or softly beatboxing—which seemed almost as vital to her as breathing—there had always been a hardness, a protective shell. I had not known it until when, for a moment, lost in memory, the fierce self-protection unexpectedly sloughed off.

"He took me to a cave—" she began. I couldn't help it; I broke down laughing. Zoraida looked up sharply, readily on the defensive again, and then she broke down into helpless laughter as well. We both laughed until, if we'd been kee, tears would have been pouring down our faces. No tears for us, but gasping in uncontrolled shared hilarity was close enough to being human again.

Zoraida was truly becoming a friend now. I had thought of her as a friend before—and when I was am'r-nafsh, she was one of the few who could be trusted to be alone with me and not try to drain me of my delicious am'r-nafsh blood. Among the am'r that is a rare thing. But I had some notion of how closed-off she kept herself, and the unevenness of the relationship had caused me a slight discomfort, knowing that no matter how open I held myself to her, she held herself firmly shuttered, against all, including me. That she was choosing to open up so widely now filled me with a deep, humble happiness.

"*Wi, wi,*" she wheezed, trying to get control over the last paroxysms. "Am'r always do end up in caves, *se vre.* But caves are so good at keeping out all the daylight, *non?* And they are not *flammable;* you do not want to be an am'r in a hut of wood and mud walls and grass-thatched rooves with your enemies around you with torches.

"It was not so far away, this refuge and that was very good, for the rising sun was already making Kgosi wince with pain when we reached it. We rushed inside, my hang-over making me as glad for the cool darkness as he.

"Upon stepping in, the entrance zone was filled with the remains of long-dead animals and seemed very unwelcoming, as did the next open area after it. On the far side of that was a hidden opening, where I found a well-appointed little chamber, with a comfortable old bed in the style of a century past with smooth cotton sheets and a bookshelf filled with works in French, Latin, Greek, Spanish, and English. Only the homes of our richest, most powerful leaders could boast a library such as this, and here it sat, cavalierly, in this cave. On a carved stand, there was a bone china basin and matching jug filled with water, soft towels set beside. There was a fancy old chair, carved and padded. And a wooden closet against one wall, softly scenting the air with cedar.

"In this small space was more luxury than I had ever experienced in my whole life until that point. Kgosi lit candles for me and after I had examined everything, I suddenly felt myself become shy. 'Come, sit down,' he invited me, and I perched uncomfortably upon the chair. He laughed at me. *Non, chouchou*, this bed is much more comfortable. Come, sit with me.'

"I forced myself over to the side of the bed and arranged a plump cushion between us. It was the first time I ever touched velvet, and I marveled at the fine nap under my fingers, using it as an excuse not to meet his eyes.

"He reached out and brushed his fingers along my cheek. It was the first time he ever touched me. I felt that touch shock along every nerve ending in my body. The little hairs on my body stood on end. My eyes flashed to his. Meeting those rich brown eyes was even more intense when his flesh was making contact with mine. I could not look away.

"And then the pillow was no longer between us, and I was in his arms, and we were kissing. I had not known kissing could be like that, as intimate as any other part of the sex act, as if we were passing our souls back and forth with our tongues.

"He moved me along slowly, pulling off my boy's clothes and kissing my body until I could not speak for lust. And then he kissed between my legs, and I found many sounds to make, some of them even comprehensible words. At some point, his kisses became bites, but those were sweet, not bitter, just another kind of kissing.

"The first time I tasted his blood was the same sensory shock as the first time touching velvet. The salt and iron and heat melted on my tongue, pure pleasure, and immediately I wanted more and more of it. That pleasure mixed with what he was doing to my body, as far from the inexperienced humping I had done before as velvet is from burlap.

"We loved each other for a long time and then we slept, and then the lust in our bodies woke us and we loved again. Again we slept, again we woke to passion. At some point I did realize that, as promised, my hangover was long gone, and my body felt as well as—no, *better* than it ever had in my whole life. I remember I smiled languorously up at Kgosi in some intermission, and joked to him, '*Yon jou pou chasè, yon jou pou jibye*'—'the hunter has his day, but the prey has his day as well.' My love looked down at me with that powerful smile and said, 'You are my prey only for a little while, *chouchou*; soon enough you will be a hunter of the whole world.'"

Remembering that, Zoraida smiled. A perfectly ferocious smile. If I were not an am'r as well, I'd have shivered like a prey animal. Kgosi's words about his frithaputhra were entirely accurate. She was not yet an aojysht, but the powerful vhoon-anghyaa of Bagamil through Asdrúbal down through Kgosi would make any am'r think twice about provoking her.

"We did not come out of that cave for a week. Well, I left it to relieve myself. And we left it together to bathe in a nearby stream and refill the pitcher for touch-up cleanings in between lengthy sessions of passion. And, while I slept, Kgosi went out to get me food, because, as you must remember, Noosh, the hunger after those first few times exchanging blood is profound.

"When we saw other people next, I was his am'r-nafsh, and bound to him by vhoon-ties as well as those of love.

"It was my first love. And my last love. I know you love Sandu and Bagamil very much, but Kgosi and I loved as no one else has loved—*hush*, do not tell me that is foolish. He is gone, so I may believe it. For most, whether they have lost their patar or not, an am'r moves on to take an am'r-nafsh of their own. In time, they will have made multiple frithaputhra, and that love strengthens an am'r as the centuries go by. To know that you have given those you hold dear the chance of eternal life, to know that although you may go your own ways, they are out there in the world, vhoon-connected to you forever and that you may chance across them again (for the world is strangely small), that is a comfort for most am'r. But not for me. Once I lost Kgosi, the thought of such intimate connection with another sickened me. Not only did I not want it, I did not feel I could even physically commit the act; in my heart, it would have been the grossest sacrilege.

"When we left the cave together, I was but the newest am'r-nafsh, but I was also now a stronger helpmeet to my love, for I had greater strength to fight by his side and my blood would sustain him better than any kee. It is, I know, a situation you find all-too-familiar...."

"Yes! It's crazy to hear this, Zoraida! Everyone made such a big fuss of Sandu not hiding me away, 'as all am'r do with their am'r-nfash'"—I may have sounded more than a little bitter as I quoted this—"but Kgosi didn't hide *you* away. And you were in the middle of a war, and everything!"

"Ahhh, but Sandu is one of the most famous am'r of all time, Dracula Himself! People pay more attention to what he does; it makes more noise. You are the power-couple of the am'r world. Who were Kgosi and I? Just some *ayisyen* am'r no one had ever heard of, whom no one has heard of still. That silly story that was written was lost to time——except for the most fanatical academics of obscure vampire literature—and did not actually note Kgosi's name. It is a truth that there is no toleration for racism among the am'r—and I am pleased to have personally helped eliminate any am'r of that ilk who have made it so far, whenever I have gotten a chance—but still, there is a sort of global prioritizing of what goes on amongst the am'r of Europe and the United States over the trifling skirmishes of the brown and black-skinned ones on the edges of a Eurocentric map. I was not the first am'r-nafsh to fight by the side of her patar, and you will not be the last. I am certain that Bagamil himself, the Aojysht-of-aojyshtaish, had many am'r-nafsh who went through the world with him. *He* never told Sandu, his own frithaputhra, not to bring you out into the am'r world. *Sètènman*, it is safer to keep your am'r-nafsh hidden away. But not all of us have that *privilege*...."

I sighed. "I wish that was surprising. I just could have done with less pearl-clutching about Sandu bringing me along with him—it added so much confusion to what was already bewildering enough for me. But, looking back, I realize *you* never seemed surprised about it."

"*Men wi non!* Another reason Sandu and I have been such friends; I never gave him shit about that choice. Other choices, *well*..." Zoraida winked at me, and I grinned back at her, adoring her entirely.

"I should finish my story before it is time to rest for the day. We have a few more days of travel until we arrive; however, I do not want to drag this out. It is one thing unlocking these wounds for one night, but I do not want to keep reliving this pain so deeply night after night. I have spent enough years doing just that.

"So, as I was saying, back out into the world we went. As you can imagine, I was rested and refreshed as I had never felt before in my life. And my vhoon had reinvigorated Kgosi, so that his beauty glowed almost like a nimbus around him. I couldn't imagine how anyone thought he was an ordinary mortal. But then I thought of *Madanm* Sanité and her comfort with the knowledge of his otherness, and how there was not one fighter who would not rather have the *lwa* helping them out in person. He was touched by the gods, and he was on our side. That was enough.

"You might wonder, if Kgosi and I were out fighting the *maren* with the Cacos, why did we not beat them back easily? How could we fail against mere kee?

"But, as in times past, we were not the only am'r in *Ayiti*. This time of chaos had been like honey to flies for those am'r who love brutality and who meet their needs for sadistic viciousness by following the never-ending wars around the world. Under cover of kee atrocities, they could get away with almost anything without risking adharmhem and the wrath of the other am'r.

"Ouiliyanm was one of their number. He was a *yanki* am'r, Sergeant Dorcas Lee Williams. 'Ouiliyanm' was what he came to be called as rumors spread around the countryside that he terrorized. I do not know how he had managed to work it so that he was in their military, for military lives and am'r lives are not particularly compatible, but many a serviceman has found that long service in a distant land means getting away with behavior that would not be acceptable back home.

"There were other am'r to be dealt with, but Ouiliyanm was the most powerful. He had strong mesmerism over his kee subordinates, and he created am'r who were subservient to him both within the ranks, and in the *Gendarmerie d'Haïti*, the *ayisyen* who sold out to the *maren* and did their dirty work for them. Ouiliyanm knew well what a threat Kgosi was, and he would often commit his carnage far from us. By the time we arrived at his latest horror, he would be elsewhere inflicting his dirty deeds on some other farmers he decided "looked like Cacos" or beating women to death because they would not tell him the location of local hideaways. He left a trail of lynched men up and down the area he effectively 'ruled.' If you go to those towns today, there is still a collective memory of Ouiliyanm as the worst sort of bogeyman, one who was once more than just a fairytale to scare children.

"We hunted after him, anger at his atrocities fueling night-long rides on stolen horses or waiting in ambushes that turned out to be exhausting but fruitless.

"And sometimes we found him. More than once we battled him, exchanging gunfire until our ammunition ran out, then Kgosi met him amidst the bodies, crashing swords together, until both am'r were wounded terribly. Yet neither could get the upper hand. They were too evenly-matched, strength against strength. In the end, the surviving Cacos and *maren* would flee in their separate directions, and eventually both Ouiliyanm and Kgosi would sustain such injuries that they could only retreat to heal and try again another night.

"Kgosi fought and killed any number of am'r in that time, some of whom were temporary allies with Ouiliyanm, although most were solitary opportunists. I myself had even killed a few, with his help. It was only Ouiliyanm who Kgosi could not get the better of, no matter what we tried.

"Ouiliyanm had spread his own am'r-nafsh around the island. The few times Kgosi left me alone was when he went to go dispatch them. 'It is ugly work,' he would tell me. I of course would tell him I had seen many ugly things, and was not afraid. "*Non*,' he would say, in that tone of voice which I knew meant his mind was made up and there was no changing it. 'I have seen far worse than you, and it still pains me to do this thing. I will not have you part of it.'"

"Whoa—" I hated to interrupt, but couldn't help myself. "Kgosi was killing am'r-nafsh?" Having so recently been in that delicate condition myself, it really hit home.

"*Wi.* Ouiliyanm was such a threat to us all, that the only way forward was to do everything in our power to weaken him. And the way he treated his am'r-nafsh as disposable minions was reprehensible, disgusting. It is both traditional and *logical* to have but one am'r-nafsh at a time. It is a connection that must be honored while it is extant; it is an all-too-transitory state, fleeting for both the am'r and the am'r-nafsh, as you have learned the hard way, *zanmi mwen.* Ouiliyanm leaving his various am'r-nafsh untended, using them to refuel himself on their special vhoon or to do his dirty work...it was disgusting, making a mockery of the sacred process. Not that *that* made it a good thing for Kgosi to hunt them down, denying Ouiliyanm their benefits, but one reason to keep your am'r-nafsh close is for just that reason—while they are a strength, they can also be a weakness. Ouiliyanm had invested time and vhoon in making them. With each one Kgosi found and gave an early tokhmarenc, it was a true loss for our enemy. He either had to do without that extra-restorative vhoon or take the time to create a new am'r-nafsh. It was a distraction. And it made him angry, which we hoped would lead to him making mistakes. It may not seem much, but it shows how very desperate it all was at the time."

I felt it certainly *did* show that. "It must have been hard on Kgosi, knowing his own am'r-nafsh was alone, as he, um, did those things." I didn't want to think too hard about it, but if you killed an am'r-nafsh, they would just rise as an am'r, unless you burned them down to nothing but ash. Decapitation may have been enough, but it always paid to be thorough with am'r. *How ugly this life can be.* "Couldn't he have taken Ouiliyanm's am'r-nafsh and turned them to his own?" I'd heard of that being done, in at least one case. And I'd been threatened with it myself not too long ago. Not a memory I wanted to do anything with but *repress.* But I knew such things were possible.

"Do you think Kgosi could have handled all those am'r-nafsh? To start, they did not have their first vhoon-bond with him. I have heard of am'r taking on another's am'r-nafsh, but it is not a common thing, and I do not know how one overcomes the initial vhoon-bond. Should Kgosi have stolen them and stuffed them into a cave with me? *I* could never have soothed them, for I was no more experienced in the ways of the am'r. And with their bond to Ouiliyanm, would he not have found us very quickly? All of Kgosi's little sanctuaries would have been lost to us. That would have *weakened* us, not strengthened us. Maybe, given years, that would have been a worthwhile plan. But we did not have years. Every night was critical."

I sighed. "I'm sorry, Zee. I didn't think it through." Proof yet again that living in the am'r world was always a bit more than I could handle. That every time I thought I'd been shocked past ever feeling such weak-minded distress again, something would always come along and make me realize how innocent and ill-prepared I was. Sandu and Bagamil still had so much to teach me, and I—perhaps reaching new levels of idiocy—had chosen to wander off from that education and protection.

"*Non, non.* You are still so new to this world. I do not think you ever had to make such decisions, back in your old life. And it was not a step Kgosi took lightly, nor did we not both feel regret. As I say, it was a measure of how desperate things were.

"The U.S. Occupation of *Ayiti* lasted nineteen years. We fought side-by-side through them all, sometimes feeling victory was so close, sometimes holding each other through the day to stave off despondency.

"In the final years of the *okipan Ameriken*, news of the disgusting and criminal behavior of the *maren* began to trickle back to the United States. We *ayisyen* had been telling them about it for years, but it was not until *yanki* voices told the stories that people in power began to listen. Not because they actually *cared*, but because it could negatively impact the reputation of their country around the world. As word came down that the Occupation would soon be drawing to a close and that the more excessive behaviors would no longer be tolerated, Ouiliyanm became more and more depraved. As desperate as he had made us all, he was himself desperate not to leave this cozy dominion he had made for himself. He could do whatever he liked, unchecked and unworried—except for Kgosi, who kept on him like a gadfly, making him pay anyway he could for each atrocity he committed. If he could just get Kgosi out of his way, and if he could stay on in *Ayiti*, well, his wicked desires could always be sated and he could wield power through the officials both *yanki* and *ayisyen*, whom he had mesmerized or otherwise corrupted over the years. Ouiliyanm had become too spoiled, too debased, to go back to trying to live in more civilized places where he did not have such control. Any am'r who met him would soon decide to execute him under the right of adharmhem, for his behaviors would bring far too much attention to the am'r...anywhere *except* where atrocities were daily occurrences."

Zoraida stopped. Her face was drawn, with that greyish hue you see on am'r who are deeply upset or injured. "Ahhh, we come to the hard part, *zanmi mwen*. Before I start that, let me say that the nineteen years I had with Kgosi were the best of my life, despite the fact that we were fighting not just the monstrous Ouiliyanm, but the much larger monster of the U.S. Marine Corps and all the evil intent behind them from the United States, wishing to make us slaves all over again. I have seen *terrible* things all over the world, perpetuated by am'r and kee alike, in the years since then, but in a way, nothing was or can be worse than what has been done to *my* people, the people of my kee life. However, all that said, every day I was with Kgosi, we found joys in each other and in the world, we found reason to love life through our love for each other.

"We could be sitting, hiding in wait under some low trees, and a sudden rainstorm would break over us, and then we'd find ourselves kissing in the warm downpour, feeling our bodies wet against each other, looking up through the rain on the leaves and seeing rainbows in the moonlight through the raindrops. I can remember the droplets making his skin look as if it were bejeweled. The fact that at any moment we could be fighting for our lives only made it more intense, that joy and that beauty.

"And we were of one mind. *Sètènman*, we had little disputes, mostly about Kgosi trying to protect me and me demanding that I did not need such protections...but with any true concern we shared the same purpose, goals, and vision for the future. Seldom has there been such a unification of two minds. And that spilled over to our fighting. When Ouiliyanm was on the field of battle, Kgosi made me leave, or at least do my fighting as far away from him as possible. But when it was kee, or lesser am'r, we fought in a most beautiful and fatal harmony. None could stand before us: they fled or they died. Before, Kgosi was a mythic hero to my people. But soon enough, it was Kgosi-and-Zoraida, the lovers who battled the Occupiers together. A most romantic story, for a people who needed—What? You look confused. Oh! Delivrans, the boy fighter? He disappeared after I became am'r-nafsh. I no longer needed that protection. What kee could harm me, with my new strength and Kgosi at my side? And the boy-clothing would not have fooled an am'r—one sniff and they would know I was a female, an am'r-nafsh, and, if their esteshcinasti was keen, specifically of Kgosi's vhoon-anghyaa."

Zoraida hesitated. "*Bon*, I can put this part of the story off no longer... On the night when it happened, we were full of hope that this was the moment we would finally achieve victory over that monster. We had information that Ouiliyanm and a troupe of *maren* would make a sunrise attack on a Cacos village. We made our plans. The women and children quietly snuck off bit by bit during the day, pretending to be getting water from the river and gathering food and wood. Cacos, dressed in the women's clothing, returned from those errands, and then did the women's work. It looked much like daily life, for they were relaxed, laughing and teasing each other about what scrawny women they made. Inside the huts, however, were piled their machetes and all the guns we could lay our hands on.

"Our enemies had lookouts on the village all day, and maybe they should have realized the children were all gone, but the *yanki* are not always the smartest, while at the same time always smugly assured of their superiority to the 'natives.' The Cacos had a fun day of playing dress-up and cooking themselves a big meal. It was the best they'd eaten before a fight in quite a while. And then they had all night to rest and wait for the attack. They all sneaked out of the huts under the cover of darkness, so that when the bulk of the *maren* came that morning to set fire to them, or to burst the doors down looking for women to assault, they would find them empty and their adversaries at their backs and at the ready.

"It was so well-planned. It should have gone so well. But it was not just the evil Ouiliyanm leading our enemies that day. There was another am'r we called Linx—known as Commandant Freeman Lang to the *yanki*—who was in charge of the *gendarmerie*. From them, he had gotten word of our planned counter-offensive, and he had used his am'r strengths to find our men hiding in the nighttime forest. He informed his soldiers where to find their best advantage against them.

"In consequence, it was a massacre of the Cacos. Before the expected sunrise attack, a small group of *maren* made their way, a little too noisily, towards the village. They were only there to calm our expectations and keep us distracted from the other *maren* where we did not expect them.

"Linx had mostly stayed in the cities, not riding out into the countryside to do his murder as was Ouiliyanm's habit. Two such powerful am'r often stay apart, not finding cooperative alliance an easy thing. As we say, '*De kòk kalite pa rete nan menm baskou*'—'Two good cocks do not stay in the same farmyard.' But they both wanted to crush the Cacos in one thrust, and to finally eliminate Kgosi, who was a thorn the side of any who was not fighting for *Ayiti*.

"Kgosi was following Ouiliyanm. His own goal that night was in line with Ouiliyanm's desire to finally finish the business. There was plenty of work for the other Cacos and me, dealing with the kee *maren* and *gendarmerie*. As usual, I had been instructed to stay as far away from Ouiliyanm as possible, and to go and hide if he seemed to become interested in me. That always stung my pride. I had many fantasies of killing him by myself and presenting his head to my love...but, as I say, our thoughts were harmonized, and I knew Kgosi was right that I was not strong enough, not yet. It was satisfying enough to get my revenge on the *yankis* and the *kolaboratè*. We had many years ahead of us, full of

Kgosi teaching me and our shared vhoon-vayon making me stronger, so I could afford to wait.

"But Linx found me. Suddenly, all our plans were in ruins.

"I was waiting with a group of Cacos, strung out behind trees around the village. We'd put out some sentries, of course, but we were not expecting our enemy from any direction except the one in which they were demonstrably coming, walking just heavily enough to keep our attention, but making it seem like they were trying for stealth and failing—which was not unrealistic for *yanki*. Linx had brought some of his *gendarmerie*; they could move more quietly in the forests in which they had grown up. Linx, of course, had the quick and quiet am'r skills, and it was without any warning that he was behind me. I was painfully and abruptly disarmed. He held me in an iron grip, his breath on my neck as he hissed, 'Ahhhh, the infamous Zoraida, lady-fighter, Kgosi's most-beloved. It's my lucky day. And not yours, not at all.'

"'Let me go and I will fight you fairly, and we shall see about that,' I said to him, but he just laughed.

"'Why let you go when I can just drain this sweet vhoon that is calling to me, without all the fuss?' Linx was stronger than I—a bigger, thickly muscled body, and of course most importantly, he was full am'r, and I only am'r-nafsh. But I had practiced with Kgosi, how to get out of the hold of a stronger, larger opponent. And he didn't want to just snap my neck, and that hindered him.

He had his right arm around me, holding my left arm, pinioning my right simultaneously. His left hand had grabbed the top of my head, pulling it down and exposing my neck. I could feel his erection digging into the small of my back. It was a moment when, despite his superior hold on me, he was just distracted enough for me to use my own physical advantages. I stepped forward with my left leg and dropped, trying to flip him over me. It almost worked for a moment, but he realized what I was doing and threw his weight back in time. That was fine, however, for I continued dropping my head down, then threw it back suddenly, breaking his nose.

He was no longer used to his victims fighting back, and he howled every swearword in a soldier's dictionary and his grip on me loosened. I threw myself down, rolled, and came up ready for whatever came next.

"I had not called for help, but Kgosi *knew*. Maybe he heard the sounds of our fighting, or maybe he felt it through the vhoon-connection, for the next moment he was there. He did not speak to Linx nor to me, just launched himself with the momentum from his run and came down upon Linx like a stooping hawk.

I watched as they fought bare-handed, a fight like I had never seen. With Ouiliyanm there had always been almost a formality in their fights, they used weapons and kept a certain distance, dancing in to inflict injury, and then spinning out again. Now, Kgosi was just *on* Linx, and they were rolling on the forest floor, trying to rip each other apart.

"I collected my gun and my machete, but I could neither get a clear shot nor were they holding still long enough for me to reliably get a good slice out of Linx. I stuck the gun in my waistband (I was not dressed so very differently than when I had been Delivrans; it was most practical in a fight) and held my blade at the ready, trying not to feel useless.

"'*Ale! Ale! Ale!*' Kgosi yelled at me. 'Get out of here!' But I didn't want to leave him. They fought so fast it was hard to follow them in the blue-grey pre-dawn. I guess I should say that the fighting was now chaos all around us. My resistance to Linx had not been quiet, and Kgosi and Linx were making enough crashings and thrashings to wake the whole forest. Cacos and *maren* had found each other between the trees, and their whole planned attack on the village, and our little surprise for them--all of that was lost and forgotten as men battled each other through the dense forest.

"The *maren* had brought torches, for the purpose of burning people alive inside their own huts and leaving the charred remains of the village as a warning to all. These were now used as weaponry, and soon led to fires catching in dried undergrowth and last year's leaves. This was not an aid to visibility. The smoke and shadows were confusing, dancing distractions, as likely to be nothing as to be some- one coming with your death on their mind.

"I remember Kgosi rolling in a forward tumble, so that finally they were off the ground. He kept the momentum going, slamming Linx into a tree and stunning him for an instant. I dove forward and sunk the tip of my machete through his stomach until it stuck in the tree.

"Kgosi shoved me backwards. '*Non! Ale!* This has gone wrong. Get somewhere safe and wait for me!' He yanked my machete out of Linx's torso, and brought his arm back, preparing for the final swing of decapitation. But Linx threw himself forward, his left arm flying up to check the movement, which Kgosi had committed all his momen- tum to. With that blocked, his other arm flew to Kgosi's neck. 'You'll find Linx does not die as easily as all that,' he sneered, leaning his weight forward so that Kgosi stumbled back.

"At this moment, I was distracted as a *maren* crashed into me, running to the action or away from it was unclear. I used his impetus to spin him around, dropping him to his knees, and then bringing my clasped hands down with much force on the back of his neck. He fell, and if he was not dead, he would never walk again.

"'*Ale!*' Kgosi gasped to me. He had backed up enough to loosen Linx's stranglehold, and he punched him in the not-yet-healed stomach wound, dropping Linx again. 'I will come to you after I kill this one!'

"I did not like it, but my love had given more than one am'r their tokhmarenc in the time I'd known him; I must trust him. I turned and slid between the trees, headed to Kgosi's closest sanctuary, in the foundations of an old plantation the forest had swallowed up over the years. I figured as I went I could give aid to any fellow Cacos I came across.

"And so I did. I came up behind one *maren*, distracted by trying to dodge a machete, and killed him before he ever knew I was there. Looking up, I saw it was a friend who had been fighting him. We nodded to each other and I told him, 'Go, gather up everyone and get them away. This is not a good fight.'

"Occasional gunfire echoed through the forest, but it was still too dark, and the fighting was mostly too close for anyone's guns to be useful except to give a pistol-whipping. The sound of increasing wildfire was louder, and more distractingly worrisome.

"A few yards further, I came across a *maren* just as he used a trench knife to disembowel a Caco. A rush of red anger overtook me before the smell of filthy death even reached my nose. I stepped out into the small space between trees, and said to the *yanki*, 'You have murdered your last *ayisien, chen sal.*'

"That is when another scent hit me, over the blood and bowels of the dead man at my feet. I *knew* the stench of this vhoon-anghyaa. I had smelled it from a distance. I had smelled it on my love after too many fights with *him*. With Ouiliyanm.

"The *maren* who stood there with Cacos' blood on his hands was Ouiliyanm himself.

"What could I do but hide my fear under anger. And it was not that hard. '*Ou! Se yon ravet fout sal ou ye!* Come here so I may kill you, not before time!"

"'You are most ambitious, Kgosi's-get. But since your patar has failed to kill me for all these years, I do not think you will do it now, not with that rusty old pistol and your little am'r-nafsh hands.' He leered at me, and I felt a rush of furious heat at how unafraid he was of me.

"And another heat, that of humiliation. Kgosi had drilled into me so many times to keep my nose open, had worked with me to train my esteshcinasti, particularly with regards to this one vhoon-anghyaa. *Li santi fò*, He stank, a strong stink. Yet, in the heat of the moment, I had missed it. The shame of my failure was overshadowed by my immediate danger, however.

"'I have been looking forward to meeting you, sweet little am'r-nafsh. You have some powerful vhoon-anghyaa running through your veins. It will be very good for me, so thank you for bringing it here and laying it at my feet.'

"I finally found my words. 'I have brought nothing to you. I will never be yours in any way. But I *am* ready to put you down, more than ready, *vakabon*.'

"He laughed at me. 'You throw your rough creole words at me, thinking I haven't learned them. But I know many languages; this pidgin wasn't hard to learn. I have sweeter words for you: *pitit tig se tig*—you're a little tiger, just like your patar. Look at you, hissing at me like an angry cat, when I can break you with one hand. No fear, little tigress, huh? Well, I've hunted tigers in my time, and I'll show you their skins on my floor. Stop trying to scratch me, and I'll make you my pet. It is better than the alternative.'

"'*Non.* I prefer the alternative,' I told him, and drew my gun and fired, but he had moved too quickly. My bullet never touched him. He was upon me, knocking the gun out of my hand with a blow that broke my thumb.

"I had thought Linx was strong, but Ouiliyanm was even stronger. Before I could react, he spun me around, and had one arm holding both of mine down at my sides. I tried a few of the tricks Kgosi had taught me for fighting against his greater strength. They had worked with Linx, but Ouiliyanm just laughed and tightened his arm so inexorably that my own left arm felt an abrupt shooting pain and then wouldn't work properly. I told myself: I must be smart and try to find an advantage when he had let his guard down. That was the only way I could hope to get out of this, no matter what brave words I had thrown at him.

"'If you're done discovering that I'm too strong for you, let's go find your patar, little tigress. I think he'll be quite interested in talking to me *now*, don't you?'

"Ouiliyanm frog-marched me back in the direction I'd left Kgosi. He seemed to know exactly where he was, even when I didn't, and it burned me that his esteshcinasti was so much stronger than mine, that he had that deeper connection to my love.

"As we drew closer to where Kgosi and Linx had been fighting, I was dismayed to see (and hear and smell) the fire in this part of the forest was quickening around us. That equally serious threat tugged at my attention when I needed all of it for Ouiliyanm.

"Kgosi was again bodily under Linx, I saw as we stepped into the narrow clearing. They were fighting with just as much raw ferocity as when I'd left. Yet more anger and shame rushed through me, hotter than the ever-increasing fire around us, that Kgosi had counted on me getting safely away—and here I was, bringing even more worry and danger directly to him.

"Linx looked up as Ouiliyanm forced me forward through the trees. He grinned hugely. "Well, nice timing, Sarge! I'm just about to finish this uppity nigger. Then we can have some fun with his pretty little bitch—"

"In the moment of Linx's distraction, Kgosi pulled his right arm out to the side with a speed surprising even for an am'r, and *whooshed* it into that gut-wound he'd hit before, which had barely started healing, with remarkable force."

Zoraida was, probably without realizing it, acting out the movements for me with her arms. The past was present for her again in its intensity.

"Linx looked startled. As he opened his mouth, blood poured out of it like a burst damn. Kgosi yanked his head hard to the left to avoid being blinded by the gush of blood, and as Linx fell forward, Kgosi fluidly rolled in such a way that he was cuddled up to Linx's side. Kgosi raised himself up on one knee, grabbed hold of Linx's head with both hands. The movement ended with a quick, hard *cronch* of vertebrae. Linx went limp. He was not dead like a kee would have been, of course, but he was out of the fight for the immediate future, and hopefully we would shortly get back to bringing him his long-overdue tokhmarenc.

"Kgosi dropped the insensate Linx and forced himself upwards. He was cut from Linx's hits and abraded from the detritus of the forest floor. A long split on his forehead was just starting to heal but had bled as headwounds do. The area around his left eye was swelling. There was blood on much of his clothing—how much of it was his I couldn't guess. He was trying to slow his breathing, and trying to move as gracefully as usual, but, having trained with him in fighting, I could see how much it was a struggle.

"Ouiliyanm, old foe of many fights over many years, could see it too.

"'Are you sure you have the strength left to fight me? I'd hate to be disappointed by killing you too easy. Why not go rest up for our dance? Leave this little tigress with me—I'll make sure she has a good time.'

"'*Kite'l ale!*' Kgosi was so angry, he'd forgotten English.

"'I'm sure you understand that I *won't* be letting her go. Well, unless you've gotten your breath back and are ready to do-si-do with me?'

"'I have been ready to give you your tokhmarenc all these years. I am glad now is the time. Let her go and we will finish this.'

"'It's about time; I was getting worried you'd turn out to be *shy*.' Ouiliyanm sneered at Kgosi. Then he turned the scorn to me, 'Don't you plan on leaving this li'l party, sweetheart—' and with that he shoved me down. I fell on the side that had both the broken thumb and the broken arm. Neither would support my weight, and I landed badly. As I sprawled beside him, trying to get up with my good arm, he snapped a kick out with the side of his foot and caught my leg at the knee. I felt things go very wrong with the bones, muscles, ligaments, and knew I would not be walking on that leg anytime soon.

"Kgosi was already preparing to rush Ouiliyanm, but my cry of pain spurred him on. In a few steps he built up as much momentum as he could. Just before he hit Ouiliyanm, he dropped his shoulder and slammed into Ouiliyanm's solar plexus.

"Ouiliyanm was knocked back a few steps, and before he could recover, Kgosi was up within range to do a full haymaker, all his weight behind it.

"The sound of Ouiliyanm's jaw breaking could be heard over the cracking of the fire around us, and the shouting and gunshots in the near distance. I thought the whole world might have heard it.

"Ouiliyanm spun wildly, throwing his arm out as he came back around. In unlucky chance, that hand caught Kgosi's face, and while I did not hear his nose break, the blood that started gushing over lips and chin and throat was evidence enough.

"Ouiliyanm, still off balance, tried to follow with more blows, but Kgosi dodged them. Both fighters were fully focused now, as if the pain had brought them to a place of ultimate intensity. For a few minutes, they were indeed doing the dance that they had done so many times over the years, skill equal to skill. Normally they were dodging and weaving, each strike anticipated and blocked. But this was not what neither of them wanted; both were ready for this dance to be *ended*, one way or another. So they just ate blow after blow, strikes which would have taken down a weaker am'r, or killed a kee right out. Their faces were battered and swelling, blood getting in their eyes or making good shots slide off from where they landed, blood spraying along with the direction of the blow.

"Kgosi landed a strike to Ouiliyanm's neck that must have made breathing difficult. Ouiliyanm staggered and dropped. He did not go completely down but caught himself with his hands. After an instant's pause, he impelled himself back up, throwing a handful of dirt into Kgosi's face.

"Blinded, Kgosi took a step back, using one hand to try and wipe his face clean of the mingled mud of blood and soil. Ouiliyanm took this opportunity to knock Kgosi back, and he landed hard against a tree. Kgosi slumped against it, as if the tree was the only thing holding him up.

"I was afraid for him, but with the tree at his back, Kgosi could defend himself even though he could barely see. His strikes kept doing more and more damage to Ouiliyanm, and I began to hope that he would soon thrust himself off the tree and finish Ouiliyanm, for once and for all.

"Ouiliyanm, frustrated with the barrage of pain, grabbed Kgosi's hands to make it stop. Kgosi, without pause, drove a knee upwards between Ouiliyanm's legs, and I couldn't help but cheer as Ouiliyanm dropped heavily to the ground. Kgosi swung forward over him, hammering down on Ouiliyanm's spine with fists joined, as he'd taught me so effectively.

"Ouiliyanm contracted for a moment under the bombardment, then surged upwards with his arms around Kgosi's legs. He threw Kgosi bodily over himself. Unable to protect his head in time, Kgosi landed badly. In one instant I went from cheering to silent terror.

"As Ouiliyanm lurched heavily to his feet, Kgosi twitched his arms helplessly. He couldn't rise. That landing could only have broken his neck. His face, under a mask of grime, wore an expression of terrible pain.

"Ouiliyanm, no grace left in his movements, clomped over to the fire, now perilously close around us. He pulled a branch from a tree with rough force, put the tips in the fire until they caught, and came limping back with a brightly burning torch. He thrust it against Kgosi's face, and then his body, over and over again."

Zoraida caught her breath in a sob but forced the next words out. "I will not repeat to you that sight, but I burn along with every second of it in my memory. I felt every spasm of agony along with my love. I will never stop hearing the screams, and then, worse, when the screams *stopped* and I suddenly felt my Kgosi, the other half of me, was gone forever, and what was left was just a body burning down to a pile of ashes, to be lost in the ashes of the forest burning around us.

"We were all in danger of becoming the same. I would have welcomed it—to end as my love had just done. Our shared beliefs comforted us that when we died, we would return to Africa and be born again, back where we belonged. I was crazed in that moment, and that was all I desired, above all else.

"And I would take Ouiliyanm with me, if I could. *Not* to rebirth in Africa—of course not—but to whatever hell a *blan* such as he must surely go to when they die. I forgot my broken limbs and launched myself at him. It was not hard for him to knock me aside, as if I'd had no training at all. I could not see for my tears, but I blindly tried, over and over, to rip him apart, with my one good arm, the other flopping beside me painfully as I tried to find some balance.

"Ouiliyanm was slowed down by my useless attacks. Not much, but enough to irritate him. Finally, he simply dragged me off, like I was already dead. I tried to fight him with my good arm, tried to slow us down with my good leg, but he laughed in his terrible way and kept going. I screamed and screamed, but all the Cacos who had been with us were dead or fled.

"He pulled me along until he found an empty den, probably of a Creole pig who had wisely fled the chaos and destruction. He pushed me inside, followed behind, and piled dirt over the opening. I tried to undo his efforts, but he hit me with a blow that knocked me unconscious for a while.

"I awoke when his teeth dug into my neck. In the rush of terror, I fought him with all the strength I had, but in the tightly enclosed space, with only two useable limbs, I could not get power behind my strikes. All I could do was try to claw out his eyes or land my elbow hard between his legs. Nothing worked, and he laughed at me again, and said, low and rough, 'My tigress to the end! Yes, don't let me down, make it fun for me....'

"That he could both bite me and speak meant his jaw had already healed, worse luck for me. I was in terrible pain, my heart a twisted knot of anguish, and my beautiful Kgosi's worst fear was coming true.

"And that was how I died the mortal death, trapped, Ouiliyanm's arms and legs wrought-iron-like around me, the feel of his teeth defiling my skin, stealing the beautiful vhoon Kgosi had gifted me with, to which he had no right.

"That is how I died. He drained me dry, drank until I felt my heart stop. That, at least, was the final mercy, when the curtain of blackness came down and took away all the pain of mind and body and heart."

Zoraida's voice had grown softer and softer, as if she was going farther and farther away. At the end, I was straining to hear her, even though I didn't want to hear those words. They seared themselves from her memory to mine, like she wrote them on my own heart with a heated blade. I'd experienced pain and loss in the last two years, but her suffering was so much worse. The worst had never truly happened to me—even with my own mortal death at the hands of the despicable Kurgan, I'd risen to a loving welcome from my beloveds. But Zoraida, this strong and beautiful soul, had truly experienced the most heart-rending loss and excruciating death. I had suffered just enough to be able to feel it all with her, deep in my core, her words changing me forever as well.

I'd thought she was done speaking. The story wasn't over, but I wasn't sure how either of us could stand any more of it. For a while, the only sound was waves crashing against the sides of the ship. I had fallen into a trance where I just floated in the shared pain, when her voice slapped me out of it.

"I do not know why he did not let me burn, like my patar, when he was done with me. I can only assume because he knew what suffering I would awake to and was cruelly pleased by the idea.

"I later found I was in the vistarascha for over a year. My injuries had been grave enough, and I know that I did not want to wake, not to a world without Kgosi. But eventually, the hunger forced my eyes open. I was still buried in that old den, although it had long ago settled around me like a grave. The jungle grows so fast that there was no sign of burning when I climbed out, wearing nothing but crusted rags and dirt.

"I hunted the woods like a thoughtless beast for days. It was a repeat of Kgosi's fraheshteshnesh, alone and unguided. I am not entirely certain of all the damage I did—the memories are fragmentary and uncertain. Mere flickers of violence

"It was Kgosi's own regrets from his brutal awakening that eventually fully awakened me. I heard his voice in my head—I did all the time at that point, he spoke to me as if he was living, constantly at my side—and I heard him tell me his story all over again. This time, his words knocked conscious awareness into me.

"I bathed and stole some clothing from a clothesline. Then I walked to the nearest town and found a rich old *blan* to feed from. I drained him and disposed of his body. I lived in his house for a few days, and washed again and again, trying to get the feeling of Ouiliyanm's grave and my own depravity off me.

"In the end, I could not find rest in my beloved *Ayiti*. I saw ghosts everywhere I looked. And—to my sick dismay—life had in no way improved. The *yanki* still occupied our country. Our leaders were still corrupt, attacking their own people, who were still held down in the worst poverty and destitution. I fled, not sure anywhere else would be *better*, but needing to get away.

"I wandered the world for a little while. Some years. I did not keep track. But then, your Sandu found me. I'm not even sure where—one of the countries around Romania, perhaps, Hungary or Bulgaria or something. I did not care where I was; I moved through the world taking frangkhilaat when I needed, feeding only for basic sustenance, never for connection or pleasure.

"Sandu was in pain at the loss of one of his fritha-puthraish, a pain that was as deep as mine—"

I *had* to interrupt her. Perhaps I would *finally* find out about that certain former lover that Sandu always refused to talk about. "What was their name? Do you remember, Zee?"

"*Kisa?*—What? Huh? Noosh, *why* would I remember the names of your patar's previous frithaputhraish? That is his job. Where was I? Ah. I had avoided other am'r like the plague. But Sandu would not let me shun his company—he kept showing up and talking to me—"

"Yeah, he does that," I muttered, pitched low so she wouldn't stop her flow of words.

"Eventually I started to hear his words, and I realized I had a friend, one who understood me. I let him bring me back to his miles of underground fortress, and over time I found a home there. He gave me plenty of space, but over the years we grew into the habit of going out to take frangkhilaat together, watching each other's backs in that vulnerable moment. Neither of us wanted to bring a kee home, so this was a wise precaution, and I was lucky to have a companion I could trust like that."

I'd heard from Sandu about this part of their history. There were details of it I wasn't comfortable with...but after Zoraida had laid her whole story in my lap like a complex, difficult gift, how could I judge her?

"So," she said, finality in her voice. "You wanted to know my story. There it is. *Dan se zo*. Teeth are bones. Bones break. We are creatures of teeth...but those break just as easily as bone."

***

I went to the saloon the next night, as soon as the sun set. I waited for Zoraida, to see if she'd want to talk again. I wanted to be there for her if any difficult feelings came up after having dived so deeply into memories. It would be my fault for waking those old pains, after all, so I wanted to make myself easily available in case I could help.

Zoraida made no appearance that night. Nor the next. Now I was torn. Should I go knock at the door of her cabin? Or should I respect her privacy, with the risk that maybe she didn't feel she *could* reach out. No—she was more than a grown woman, she was over a century old, and profoundly capable and self-aware. I just had to respect that she needed space.

By the next night I was practically chewing my nails. Nthanda wasn't leaving the captain's cabin—he just sent for sustenance (day crew) as required. Which was regularly. There really were *no* supernumerary crew on this vessel, at least not with Nthanda leaving them like empty Capri Suns. Lilani's treachery had really been hard on him; I knew he was angry at himself for not having had the slightest clue. But I wasn't sure if he was grieving—or just building up his strength for a serious campaign of vengeance. *Both*, probably.

Viv finally made an appearance, just as I was starting to think I'd go mad with lack of either information or distraction. He slid with the usual am'r grace onto a curve of the sofa, and asked, "You right, Noosh?"

I half-smiled at him. "Kinda. Not really. Do you know—do you have any idea how Zoraida is doing? We had this really intense talk, and I haven't seen her since. I'm giving her space...but I'm still a bit worried."

Viv laughed. "First time anyone I know's ever worried about *Zoraida*. Even for an am'r, that one keeps herself to herself."

Now I felt embarrassed for even bringing it up. "Oh, I *know* she doesn't really need any help from me...I just, I dunno, it's just that I do care about her, is all."

"And you're a luv for doing so, but what I was about to say is that even for someone as solitary as Madam Zee, she's not been very *lonely* these past days. I think the *Luis* has lost a crewmember, because that girl will certainly be disembarking with her at Tangiers."

"Wait—*what?*"

"You really didn't know? The crew been chinwaggin' about it endlessly. You *must* listen to gossip, if you want

to live long—more than one am'r's escaped serious bar-
ney and early tokhmarenc by listening to little voices. Apparently, the first night of this passage, Zoraida took re-
freshment from among the day crew, a new one who'd just
signed on in London, some kind of refugee. After a couple
nights, she asked for her again, and this Delicious Miss never left your poor lonely Zoraida's cabin since. Apparently,
this's caused a fair bit of shirtiness amongst the rest of
the crew, because they're all very ready for a bit of fresh
blood—get it? Ha!—to do all the grunt work. But there you
have it. If Madam Zee's feeling gutted, she's drowning her
sorrows in this kee's sweet vhoon."

"Oh." I was entirely without words. Well, apparently, I
really didn't need to worry about Zoraida. I went back to my
own problems...which I soon realized I'd been conveniently
sidestepping with my focus on Zoraida. But here I was, back
again: had I made a terrible decision by leaving Sandu and
Bagamil to go along with Nthanda to hunt Lilani? What
could have possibly made me think I was ready for this?

With such self-doubts, I stared out at the ocean and tor-
mented myself all night long.

The next night was the last of this leg of our travels. The
Luis would tie up at the port of Tangiers while we rested
during the following day, and then disembark at sunset. I
knew we were headed to another part of Africa from there,

but had not been able to get more out of Nthanda before he disappeared permanently into his cabin.

I was hoping Viv might join me again, so that I wouldn't be alone with my thoughts. I'd given up on the other two entirely, and the crew knew nothing except our immediate destination.

I sensed movement and looked up in time to catch Zoraida settling herself down, exactly where she had before. Caught entirely off guard, I blurted out, "Zee! Why are you here?" and then, mortified, I rushed to add, "Not that I'm *not* delighted to see you! But rumor has it you've found a cure for loneliness...." And then I kicked myself again. After all she'd shared with me about Kgosi, that was too flippant. *La donna* was NOT *mobile*. Nor an am'r to trifle with, even if she did consider me a friend.

But Zoraida smiled serenely at me. I'd seen her glowing with health from having vhoon-fed in the past, but now she had a look of deep satisfaction as well. *The cat who drank the cream—but of course, with the am'r, every metaphor stands in for* blood.

"You are thinking, perhaps, that I protested too much that I would never love again, *zanmi mwen*, and after all these years, I find that being foolish in love does not sting as once I might have thought."

I started to protest that no, of course she wasn't foolish, but she cut me off. "Just a few days ago, I sat here and told you that love would never find me, that I had loved once and never again. I *believed* it, too, for that way of thinking had never been proved wrong, in all this time.

"But now, with this new happiness infusing my every limb, I no longer care if I look a fool for anything I proclaimed mere days ago—or a century ago. I was lucky enough to find love then, and I am still amazed to have found love now."

I bit my tongue before, "Are you sure you're not just drunk on too much vhoon?" slipped out. I remembered how Sandu had been, when he had decided he loved me (practically at first sight), and nothing would slow down his headlong rush into convincing me I felt the same. Apart from our own am'r-and-am'r-nafsh relationship starting, I'd never seen another of these most unique forms of bonding kicking off. Maybe all am'r got "cuckoo for Cocoa Puffs" at this stage of things.

"I'm really happy for you," I said instead. "Can I meet her?

"*Sètènman!* She will have many questions for you, who was so recently am'r-nafsh. Please tell her anything you can think that will help."

"I would *love* to," I replied, and I'd never meant my words more. Just remembering all the things that Sandu conveniently *forgot* to tell me, because he thought he'd scare me off, or all the things that no other am'r mentioned to me, because they simply hadn't been kee in so long they couldn't remember ever needing such information, I resolved to set up an am'r-nafsh advice group on the am'r intranet, once I got back to Castle Dracula.

If I got back.

Ugh, don't think about that now, focus on what is right in front of you, girl. It's happiness, *for once.*

"So, uh, you met her the very first night? And I don't even know her name!"

"Her name is Ediye. It means 'beautiful,' as she is." Zoraida simply couldn't look more smug. I felt a rush of pleasure at her blissful contentment. Who could have deserved this more?

"Viv said she was a refugee? How did she end up here?"

"You know of the war Russia is making on Ukraine?"

I nodded, but honestly, maintaining an interest in the kee world was proving hard for me. I was trying to force myself to listen to the news on my phone every night, but the intense dangers of the am'r world were more immediate, more intimidating, more *real.* I'd been telling myself that staying in touch with what went on with the kee was just as important as anything else I was dealing with. Did I want to become one of those am'r who were startled by everyone suddenly having mobile phones after never having noticed the invention of the telephone in the first place? Who could not comprehend the problems of the century they were living in? If I was so afraid of becoming inhuman, I needed to grasp the nightly news with both hands; I needed to keep up with new music trends; I needed to watch the TV shows the kee were all making memes about. *I should know more about this war, dammit!*

"Ediye is Nigerian," Zoraida was telling me, and I hauled my attention back to where it belonged. "Many Africans went to Ukraine to get university degrees, and then either bring the knowledge back to help their country or get a well-paying job and send money home. She was so excited, learning to be a doctor, getting the training she needed to aid those around her in such desperate need. It was still her first year, and she hadn't settled on pediatrics or gynecology yet—both are so crucial. She loved living in Ukraine—although the winters were hard on her, she adored the people, how open and welcoming they were.

"When the war began, she couldn't believe it. Suddenly, all the safety she'd felt was pulled out from under her, and she was having to flee a war zone.

"But the worst was yet to come. She walked through freezing temperatures with only what she could carry and got to the Polish border—but she was refused entrance to Poland. She was told, 'Blacks without European passports cannot cross the border,' as she watched white Ukrainians walk past her to safety.

"She was put onto a crowded bus—and you are aware that the kee are going through another pandemic as well, *wi?* So, this in-and-of-itself is dangerous—with all the other rejected African students and workers, and they were sent to the Romanian border, where finally they were allowed to cross, where finally they were recognized as legitimate refugees from war, and not seen as opportunistic, unwelcome migrants.

"They say the world gets better over time, but this is not my experience of the kee world. The old prejudices, the old lies which are retold to keep one people down under another people reemerge in each generation. Those who fight to keep those things alive can claim more triumph than those who fight against them. It makes me wonder if Kgosi was right, and we am'r should start to intervene in the kee world, eliminate the worst perpetuators at the very least. It is something I must consider....

"But at least, for this moment, I can pull my beautiful Ediye out of that, and bring her into our world—which is not perfect, *non*, but where at least the might that makes right has nothing to do with your gender or the tone of your skin.

"You will talk with her now, *wi*? I will bring her up here? She is wary of meeting the other am'r, which is of course something I will encourage in her, but I would like her to acquire from you all the lessons you have just learned the hard way."

"Please, Zee—I am so excited to meet her and tell her everything I can think of! And I am so happy for you both!"

The joy sparkling in Zoraida's eyes gave me a contact high. And, win-win, now I had something to distract me completely from the dubious choice I'd made, from the all-too-real dangers in my own immediate future. For one last night, at least, those fears could be thrust aside, and I could enjoy being safe and surrounded by true, caring friends. And making a new friend and renewing my connection to the kee world in the process.

Tomorrow night, however, both Ediye and I would be disembarking into the terrifying next stage of our new realities. At least I could make it a little easier for her than it had been for me.

NOTE ON TEETH ARE BONES

This story was originally published in the *Together We Stand Volume 2 Charity Anthology*, in support of The Red Cross for relief in Ukraine. I came across that anthology's call for authors a few months before it was being published, and I wrote in to the wonderful people who were doing it, and said, "Oh, I've just seen this now for the first time and I'm so sorry I missed the deadline for this, but please keep me in mind for a future one!" And they wrote back, oh no, we can make room for one more story. You have a month and a half to turn your story in!"

"Oh shit!" I said out loud to myself. "What did you just do?!" But then I stopped talking to myself and started hurriedly buying books about the history of Haiti.

I always knew Zoraida was a character who was going to eventually get fully fleshed out. She had made her appearance first in *Blood Sine Qua Non*, and not only did I fall in love with her, but fans, did, too, and she won a reader poll to have her story be the one I wrote.

I wanted to tell her story right, so I watched documentaries on Haiti, read histories of Haiti, and read Haitian writers. I went from having the average American's lack of knowledge about the wonderful island of Hispaniola to having my heart broken over and over again as I learned its brutal, horrifying history. And I fell in love with the indomitable spirit of the Haitians, their gorgeous musical Kreyòl, and their amazing cuisine.

I can only hope that I have done both Zoraida herself and her beloved country justice in my telling of her story.

Here are a few of the resources I found most useful. (But first let me make very clear that if there are any mistakes in this story, they are mine and mine alone.)

Haiti: The Aftershocks of History by Laurent Dubois is extremely readable and a great starting point to get an overview of the facts by a historian who clearly cares deeply about the Haitian people.

The Revolutions Podcast by Mike Duncan is a deeper dive, and perfect to listen to when driving or cleaning the house. The Haitian Revolution starts at episode 4.0.

The Long Legacy of Occupation in Haiti, by Edwidge Danticat:

https://www.newyorker.com/news/news-desk/haiti-us -occupation-hundred-year-anniversary

I also couldn't have done this story properly without a sensitivity editor, especially one who could also correct my fumbling attempts at Kreyòl. I was very lucky that Émelyne Museaux was available to work with me, and I recommend her highly. She does narration work for audio as well! Check her out: https://emuseauxediting.com/

All the fight scenes in the story were worked out in person with Trent Stewart so that they would flow well and make sense physically, and I thank him for his time and knowledge.

This story takes place in the world of the Blood & Ancient Scrolls Series (between Book III, Blood Ad Infinitum and the upcoming Book IV, Blood Abyssum).

BLOOD BROTHERS

"Now you're all mine!" I proclaimed, beaming, as my guests entered my library.

Dubhghall looked at Wulfhram, and they laughed. Wulfhram's laugh was a deep booming of open-hearted humor, Dubhghall's was more of a chuckle and higher-pitched, as suited his smaller frame. He was the more self-contained of the pair, although the deep blue eyes were generally brightened by a roguish twinkle.

"How'd we get lifted that quick?" Dubhghall asked.

"Because you always want to talk about yourself; it is your great weakness," Wulfhram said solemnly, and shoved Dubhghall with a strength that would have knocked over a mortal human.

Dubhghall didn't show any sign of having been jostled so roughly. He just grinned back at the bigger man. "Aye, yer an awfy blether, ya bampot."

"Stop talking like that," Wulfhram chided. He turned to me, "He is just making you balance off your feet,

Frøken Noosha. He can talk in your English just as good." Wulfhram apparently had no idea that his own English was thickly accented and clearly not his first language. It's like that with the am'r. Either they can pick up new slang and other linguistic shifts as easily as breathing, or they sound like the caricature of a vampire: all stiff and formal in modern languages in which they'll never feel at home.

Dubhghall was one of the former. Now that he'd been busted, he continued in accent-less General American, "We don't mind being trapped in your lair at all, Noosh. We've heard so much about it—" I blushed, here, because *I* was the one who would babble on at endless length, if given the opportunity— "and we support this project deeply. I'm sorry it's taken us so long to get here."

"But now we are here," Wulfhram proclaimed, "Please show us around, *Frøken* Noosha."

"Just 'Noosh,' please," I insisted, as I led them in. There was nothing I was happier to do. The slowly growing am'r archives were my dream job, my pride and joy. In the past few years I'd spent too much time fighting desperately for my life, and too little settled down in this climate-controlled cave somewhere outside of Bucharest, doing what my passion and my previous life in the kee (that's "living human") world had prepared me for: organizing the am'r documents (vellum and parchment scrolls, clay tablets, codices, etc.) that had piled up, not properly cared for, for centuries—millennia, even. I was specifically trying to find any mention of "maadak," the only poison/intoxicant which worked on the am'r, and which had been the bane of my existence (well, along with certain am'r who'd used it on my beloveds and me) from the minute I'd gotten involved with the am'r. Apparently, some am'r had gone their whole existences without ever getting messed up with that stuff, but my own experience had, unfortunately, been far too full of it. Probably something to do with having accidentally hooked up with Vlad Dracula and his patar, who was the oldest and most powerful of the am'r. You just weren't taking *them* down without *cheating*.

Part of my job as am'r archivist was talking to as many am'r who would talk to me. And not all of them *would*; am'r are the most crankily solitary critters around. I was trying to collect their stories and systematize their knowledge of the aspects of am'r existence. Besides building a collective knowledge base for new am'r—a radically new idea for these misanthropic beings—there was a chance that anyone who had experiences with maadak might contribute a breadcrumb to the trail leading back to its discovery or creation. And I'd take every little clue I could get.

The downside of successfully eliminating your enemies is you can no longer question them. In particular, I wished

I could torture some information out of a certain Kurgan, now a very deserving pile of ashes. While I was relieved he was forever in the "done and dusted—literally!" state of being, I felt frustratingly certain he'd known the exact information for which I was sifting every written and spoken word.

I started them off in the display area. Our oldest, most precious, or just prettiest texts were kept in UV-filtering safety glass vitrine, with LED lighting that could be turned on when I was trying to impress an unconvinced am'r that they should trust me with their hoarded stories. I then moved them on to the scanning and restoring technology and environmental monitoring sensors: the highest end stuff, every fancy little toy to play with which this archivist could ever have dreamed. Their replies became more monosyllabically polite as I went on, but an archivist must indulge her desire to talk about document restoration whenever opportunity presents.

We hustled more quickly past the server room. My tech goddess, Zoraida, was back in Haiti, the land of her birth (both as kee and am'r), trying to help as best she could in a time of ongoing crisis from *very* behind the scenes.

We ended in possibly the most important room, the "Get Am'r to Chill" area. It was very low-light, too dark for kee eyes to find useful, but just right for am'r. In the soothing shadows, there were a variety of comfy chairs and recliners and sofas, the kind that you sink into and never want to get up from again. Am'r don't require this—we don't get muscle aches—but I still found it psychologically effective. A properly comfy chair can be appreciated by anyone, kee and am'r alike.

They settled in, not sharing a sofa, but in side-by-side chairs. Wulfhram had to adjust the sword—which had been neatly and invisibly hanging under a long, black, wool topcoat—to get comfortable. Dubhghall was undoubtedly armed as well, but not visibly. Entirely used to hanging out with armed predators, I dropped onto my favorite sofa, and grabbed a modern tablet set up for both voice recording and any jotted notes I cared to make with the sleek mechanical stylus.

"I know you are looking for a cure for maadak, but neither of us has much experience with it," Wulfhram said apologetically. "I know not how much we can help, *vinurinn*, but we are happy to try."

"I don't mind," I smiled the truth warmly at him. "I do really just want to get to know you and Dubhghall better. You were both so kind to me ever since a very stressful first day."

"It was a *heavy* first day," Dubhghall grinned. "You did not look very relaxed. Sandu can be very stupid that way.

He combined the worst parts of 'Meeting The Parents' with 'And Now We Face Our Enemies,' *plus* your first time in the am'r world. I'm surprised nothing worse happened."

"Worse than me being kidnapped?"

"We got you back—and had a little fun doing so! No, *worse* would have been if you had run screaming. We need you, but no one needs you more than Sandu. He was a miserable cunt before you came along. Very mopey, for centuries. Of course you make Bagamil very happy, too, but he's always been very...self-sufficient. Sandu, *he* needs someone to keep his head from going too far up his arse."

Dubhghall's speech was *mostly* accent-less, but hints of Scottish zest snuck back in and made me smile down at my tablet.

"It's not like I could have left, you know. I'd already been made am'r-nafsh. I was already...brought into this world." I didn't say, "trapped." It would have made me sound like I was holding on to old resentments, and truly those were blood under a bridge of bodies by now.

"Most could not have left. Perhaps *you* could have."

The compliment made me strangely embarrassed. I covered it by waving my hand around. "And leave all of *this?* No kee job could offer me anything like this."

They smiled kindly at my obsession, and I took the moment to turn them to the conversation we should be having.

"But you already know *my* story first-hand. I want to hear about how each of you became am'r, and the escapades you've had since then."

"You go first," Wulfhram urged Dubhghall.

"Fine. I do enjoy telling a tale."

Dubhghall moved his head and shoulders around slightly; I could almost see him gathering his thoughts. He was a slight man, with wiry muscles you might not notice under clothing. His skin was the shade of the vellum manuscripts in the next room. His dark hair waved in well-styled curls, adorable against forehead, ear, and neck. His eyes were so black you could not tell where the pupils began.

"I began life in one of the tribes of the Picti, as the Romans called us when they were sitting back in Rome writing their self-aggrandizing stories and not just trying to make us part of their Empire the hard way. We had many names for ourselves, and many different tribes with different traditions. It amuses me to no end when today's archaeologists try to figure us out. They end up calling us a "heterogeneous group," which translates to them not having a fucking clue. It means we were what all people are: just living our lives and evolving over time.

"We'd inhabited an area called Pictland (the Scoti were still just another tribe among many) a very long time, at least by our reckoning. Plenty of time to build strong stone houses and pass them down from mother to daughter—we were a matrilineal people, as makes the most sense—increasing our herds in times of plenty, and hunkering down with kale and parridge in leaner times. Our land is not one of gentle winds and rich fields, it is a place of craggy hills and stony beaches and bitter weather. The people are as rough and durable as the landscape. I am proud to call it my birthplace, and those people my ancestors.

"I was the son of a noble family, but your modern eyes would have noticed little difference between us and the families of lesser social status. More metal jewelry: torcs and brooches. More beads. A better weave of woolen cloth, and perhaps a brighter dye on the fabric. But us "nobles" worked as hard to ensure food was on the table. We may have hunted more, but we still had herds to care for. Our lives were not noticeably that of comfort and ease. What being noble meant was that we were the ones who trained for fighting. We could afford to commission weapons and helms from an ironsmith. We could afford to keep horses—that is, we could afford to keep animals not for *food*. Although we ate the horses when we *needed* to. This strange aversion to horsemeat is a more modern invention, a product of the Church's war on pagan customs. But we were not pagans! Saint Ninian and Saint Columba had given us a Christianity which we'd blended with our earlier traditions—and suited us very well, thank you! Although later on, the Roman Church was not quite pleased with how we did things. But that is another story.

"Invaders were part of our lives, and they either broke themselves on our coastlines and our swords, or they stayed and became part of us. And I cannot say we were not occasionally raiders ourselves. There was a very fine line between being a trader and a pirate in those days, and anyone with a boat could be one on one day and the other the next. Indeed, that is a thing which has not noticeably changed in all the years I've been on this earth.

"As I said, invaders on our shores were as much a fact of life as the weather. But, starting before my birth, incursions from the peoples who were going a-Viking began to drastically increase. It's popular now to write about the attacks by the Danes in the British Isles, but in Pictland, in the Kingdom of Fib—called Fife, these days, so I'm a Fifer!—we got Norwegians. Big blonde bawbags like him." He gestured at Wulfhram, who grinned expansively and waved like royalty on parade.

"I'll leave it to this dunderclunk of a *faol-chù* to explain why *that* was going on, but for my people then it was mostly like...I don't know...like climate change is now: worse storms, more frequently, destroying our way of life. Or just *changing* it. Sometimes those who had gone a-Viking wanted only violence and silver. Sometimes they wanted some land and a wife for their own, to settle down, and be a strong neighbor against the next group of arseholes who showed up waving swords around.

"Because of raiders who stayed, our land was multilingual. You could ride a mere ten kilometers and be speaking a totally different language—or a dialect that was becoming incomprehensible from the dialect spoken where you grew up. I was always quick with tongues—nae sniggering fae you, arsepiece!—and I picked up Norsk, the language of the Northmen, and the languages of the Scoti and other tribes. Once word of that got around, I was as requested for help with trading as often as I was with raiding.

"But as I got older, it became more an environment of increasing uncertainty. There was no monastery near us to lure the get-rich-quick kind of raiders—my people had only the riches we created from being careful herders and hunters, crafty with iron and stone, creative with wool and flax and reed. But even if we were not Lindisfarne, still our lives were disrupted over and over again. We kept watchers on the shore and along the rivers. A stranger was more likely to meet hostility than our traditional hospitality. Even if your homestead was not burned and pillaged *this time*, stories came from every direction, keeping a very real dread in all hearts.

"I'm not saying that our lives had been free of violence before the Northmen started invading our lands. Cattle-raiding was in our blood, and I'd been on more than one nighttime raid, myself. Just because we were all under the common name of "Pict' does not mean we were all unified and friendly. If we did not have external enemies to fight, we fought amongst ourselves.

"But I was in my late twenties and never unready for a fight. I spent much time sharpening my sword and dagger, boasting of feats that were hardly worth remembering. I had a spear as well, and a shield and helm. Many of the lads my age used the excuse of the raiders to spend our time riding about "on patrol." We truly *were* looking for a fight, but we were looking just as much for drinking and winching. Which would soon enough lead to a fight.

"I had more experience fighting in those cattle raids than against actual Northmen-gone-a-Viking. Oh, a few times a fire-beacon called us to a landing site, and we got to battle against raiders laden with sheepskins and food and other goods, but they were smaller ships, and the engagements were cut short by the raiders getting in their ships and sailing away. A man gone a-Viking would rather come home with their plunder than die in battle. But I thought I was a true warrior and swaggered with it.

"But then the word went out. A flotilla of Víkingr ships had been spotted in the Firth of Forth, and all trained fighters—swaggering younglings and grey-beards alike—were called into a rag-tag army. Every able-bodied man (and some women dressed as such) were called to do their duty to the King. The beacons were set alight, but it still took a while for the news to reach all the clans. It was not until a few farms were smoking piles of ash, before the raiders had already killed men, stolen women and cattle, and dug up carefully hidden personal hoards, before we caught up to them with our own army.

"The King of the Picts, Drest son of Uurad, gathered us all to him the night before we met the enemy, and he feasted us and there we drank much mead. The bards sang poems and recited the stories of warriors who had done great deeds—which we were all supposed to live up to the next day.

"Most drank to excess. It was not unreasonable to be terrified of what was to come the next day. It would be slaughter, and either you would be *doing* the slaughtering, or you would be dying an agonizing death. Unless you managed to run away, those were your only two options.

"The King and his men had us marching at dawn. I would say most of us did not set out the next morning with a hangover—but that's only because we were still drunk. Some of us were still drinking on the way! I was young enough to be more excited than scared. I truly thought I understood what I was striding manfully towards, as drunk on myths of prowess as on alcohol. I carried a sword that had been my grandfather's: perhaps seventy centimeters, so a longer short sword. It was a well-weighted weapon, and I'd been carrying her since I was old enough to move up from practice wooden swords to the real thing. She was a natural extension of my arm, and I loved her more than any woman. Her name was Pointeach—Pointy."

"You *truly* are no poet. You must be a constant disappointment to your ancestors."

"Shut yer puss, ya lavvy-heided wankstain. As I was *saying*, we marched to where the raiders had beached their ships. They'd been sending raiding parties only far enough away that they could get back to their ships at night, then guarded them through the night, and sent parties out the next day for more raiding. There must have been two hundred of them, and this was a different pattern than we'd seen before. Usually it was just one ship, and just one day of raiding. This was an organized group of several warlords working together to increase their reach, and thus their spoils.

"They had not expected Drest, our King, to gather us together so fast. And we'd caught a spy they'd sent out, which is how we knew their numbers so well. Their plan was to stay until we had raised enough men to counter their strength, and then slip back onto their ships with their ill-gotten goods and sail away before we could provide them with any real resistance.

"They had *also* been drinking all night—drinking plundered mead and beer that should have been sipped by Pictish lips—around fires roasting stolen sheep on the beach near their ships. We got to them before they were fully awake, just starting to pull on their mail shirts and find their helms through a hangover fog.

"We had archers with us, and we woke them with arrows. There was a low bluff—a sheer rockface down to the beach, riddled with caves—to one side of their chosen landing site. The archers were at the top, waiting for the signal to shoot.

"They were fewer than us, but every one of them a seasoned fighter, who'd chosen the 'Víkingr' way. Our greater numbers included men who never wanted to fight for their lives and homes until it was forced upon them, carrying not swords or bows, but small axes, sickles, and scythes; farming implements that nonetheless can be used with murderous intent.

"With all their experience, they only lost a small number of men to our archers. Their quicker-witted warriors were able to grab their shields and make patchwork shield-walls to protect themselves and others.

"But we had another use for our archers. They had pots of pitch with them, and the ones not shooting directly down to the beach had been sending fire-arrows to the ships. Those ships were at the far extent of our archer's range, but enough of the arrows had landed that it was not long before all four of the ships were sending up smoke. Every man who left the protection of the shield wall and tried to climb up the ships to put out the fire was immediately a target for our archers.

"The rest of our army was concealed in a forested area that grew up to the beach, with that convenient bluff rising up to our left. We waited until the enemy was in maximum chaos to march forward. Up until this point, all my highest military fantasies were playing out. We'd lost no men; our tactics were working just as planned. I was thrilled to a near-sexual excitement. I was too young and dumb to remember that in battle circumstances can change in an instant. In my mind, we'd already won.

"Most of our warriors had ridden the shaggy fell ponies we used for transportation. Our King and some other of the highest nobility had true horses, but regardless of their pedigree, all were tied up in a clearing in the woods well away from the action. The rocky beach upon which the

Northmen had been camping was hazardous footing for horses—any benefit from having a cavalry division would have been lost by that. And most of our training had been fighting on foot with spear and with sword. So even Drest, Son of Uurad, was afoot, leading our charge at the center, as was expected of our kings.

"When we emerged from the trees and lined up for battle, it gave the Northmen a wake-up jolt, and their leaders were finally able to organize them as a whole. Some of them kept up the attempt to rescue their ships, hiding from the archers by swimming around aft and climbing up in safety, but the rest were ordered to grab their weapons and make proper shield walls side by side with the crews from the other ships. Most had managed to more-or-less armor themselves. Faced with hand-to-hand combat, not just an unexpected wake-up call of arrows and fire, they pulled themselves together to do what they did best.

"In front of their burning ships they formed up three shield walls, and in no time they were drumming their shields. It made an impressive clamor, and gave me my first real intimation of fear.

"We had about three hundred fighters, now double their number since over twenty Vikings lay dead with arrows sticking out, and more than that number were occupied fighting fires on the ships. Even with the disparity of numbers, the Northmen were intimidating when not in rout. Every single one of them had chosen to be here, was experienced with their weapons and with fighting in what we called the *schiltron* and what they called the *skjaldborg*. Among our number maybe a hundred were like me, young men dedicated to a life of practicing with weapons and skirmishing. The rest of us were farmers and craftsmen, made strong by a life of hard work, and certainly always ready for a fight, but not trained warriors.

"It was far larger battlefield than any I'd experienced before. It was my first time smelling the scents of battle: drunken fear oozing from unwashed bodies, shit and piss, and vomited beer and mead.

"And that is where I would meet this radge wee shite. Right there in the space between the Pictish army and that Viking army. But perhaps this is the moment for him to tell how *he* got there."

Dubhghall made sounds of contentment as he settled back in the comfy chair, his work done for now. Wulfhram unsettled himself, scootching forward, awkwardly resting his large hands on his knees.

"My people love to tell a tale as much as this *miklimunnr*, here...but I have not spoken of these things, not in a very long while. Dubhghall, I do not need to tell—he already knows. And I would never talk of my past with another am'r. Maybe jokes with Sandu, but few others do I trust.

"Perhaps you will change this. But it is how am'r have always been. So I have forgotten *how* to tell stories…"

As Wulfhram paused to figure out how to begin, I really looked at him, more than just the usual impressions of "big" and "solid" and "blond" that were the obvious first impressions. His blond hair was reddish-gold, styled up in almost a pompadour. His eyes were cobalt blue, and he had hints of laugh-lines around them. He looked a bit more timeworn, his face more lived-in, than even am'r who were far older than him. But that made him seem far more approachable, less inhumanly distant.

"I was a little older than this Pict when we met. But we come from the same time. It can be rare, to find another am'r from the same time and place as you. Many ages of this world have gone by. And while my world—as one who went a-Víking—was larger than you may guess, still, the world is far bigger than I knew then. So, you meet an am'r, it is not very likely that they will be from the same time as you, or the same place in the world—"

"Assuming you don't just kill them first, without stopping to chat about all that," Dubhghall interjected with a flash of teeth too quick to be a grin.

"*Já*, assuming that. Killing people does hinder getting to know them." Wulfhram sent a smile back to Dubhghall, and his body language showed him finally relaxing. *Damn am'r. Violent murder is their warm comfy blankie.*

"So, as I say, it is rare for there to be another am'r who is from when and where you are from, who can so deeply understand you. It is rare, and therefore *we* are rare, two am'r who have seen the same things with different eyes."

"Oh, we are odd fish in so many more ways, *mo faol-chù*."

"Will you let me tell this story in my own way, *veslingr?*"

Dubhghall spread his hands in an expression of "Please do go on." Wulfhram took a deep breath.

"What I try to say is that our kee lives were not so very different. He lived in a house of stone, I a house of wood."

I stifled both a giggle and any comment about three little pigs. I caught Dubhghall's eye, and his face was unnaturally blank as well. I quickly dropped my glance down to my tablet, pretending to check that the sound recording was still running OK.

"We *Nordmenn* herded sheep and cattle. We grew vegetables and grains and supplemented with gathering and hunting. The clothes we wore were not so different, nor the armor that protected us in battle. My peoples were famed for their cleanliness and style, while his have come down through history as painted savages—" Wulfhram's eyes flicked over to Dubhghall, but the latter merely grinned and let the dig pass. "And, as my friend noted, his peoples could as well climb in a ship and sail in search of mayhem and gain.

"But my peoples took that much farther. Some of us stayed home and tended land and livestock. But many preferred to spend part of the year at sea, acquiring riches and wives and our reputations as warriors. And, at this time in our history, there was also pressure upon us. There was a ruler, an emperor named Charlemagne. He was forcing all the Germanic peoples to convert to Christianity—at the point of the sword. Saxons and other tribes fled, some to our country. At the same time, we had the problem of our own peoples growing too numerous for the land to support. As well, our traditions were that only the eldest son inherited from his father, leaving many other sons to find some other way to make their lives. Well, so it made sense for many to sail away from their homes and make new homes in a new land.

"A 'Viking' these days is a thing both romanticized and demonized. We were feared simply because we had a good strategy and were successful with it. But we were no more brutal than any other peoples of that time. We took less territory than the Romans. We made no forced conversions, like the Franks. In the lands Dubhghall here was just recounting for you, one tribe would do raiding against the other, back and forth, creating generations of blood feuds, as violent as anything the Víkingar might do. As I say, we *Nordmenn* were simply successful. *That* was our threat."

I had to interject, "But what about...berserkers?"

"Ha! The most *popular* part of the Víkingr stories." Wulfhram's face assumed a pained expression. "I wish I could tell you that it was all a silly myth, just to get everyone to *stop their jaws* about it.

"But...it is not a myth, and it is part of my tale. *Our* tale." He stopped talking, and there was a too-long pause.

"I'm so sorry I interrupted you! Please, Wulfhram, go back to telling it your own way."

"*Nei, nei.* I was just gathering my memories. It is good.

"I was one of those not-eldest sons. My mother was a second wife, a Saxon. That is why my name is Wulfhram. I was named for my father, but his first son had taken his name and was already the next Ulfr Ulfsson, so I was named in the language of my mother. My name means 'Wolf-Raven.'

"As a second son, it was easy to choose to go a-Víking. I had been doing it for some years and I was good. I was adept with sword and with oar. I could hold strong in a shield-wall. I enjoyed caring for the horses. I could carry heavy loads back to the ship. I was good at all the parts of Víkingr life.

"Áleifr Ulfsson was my lord. He was my uncle as well, but I was given no special favor. He had overseen my early training with the sword when he was home over the winters. It was no surprise to him when I said I wanted a place on his ship. And it was the life for me: much action, but a high regard for both strength *and* cunning. And much drinking and much fucking."

"Still your preferred life," Dubhghall noted, amused.

"*Já*. And yours, *miklimunnr*. I did not interrupt *your* tale."

"I seem to recall a comment about perpetually disappointing my ancestors. But go on."

"I think I have told enough of *who* I was. Of *how* I got there. I mean, there, across from an unruly mob of little dark men in gaudily-dyed wool and—"

"Wait!" I was too excited to care about interrupting the flow of the story. "Hold on a sec! Everything I've read says the Picts fought *naked*. They didn't?"

"Not in my experience. But ask the Pict." Wulfhram shrugged.

"This is what I mean about archeologists and historians being fucking useless." Dubhghall's tone was pure annoyance. "They can't even figure out something as *simple* as that. You can't *both* say we fought stark naked, but *then* have examples of our helms in your museums."

"So, what *did* you wear into battle?"

"The answer is 'both-and.' My ancestors traditionally did not wear much armor, which the Romans in their mail, scale, and plate armor thought proof of our barbarian madness. But we were fighters who counted on maneuverability, and we could run rings around the slow Roman tortoises. The Romans considered not wearing armor to be 'naked,' which is part of how that myth was started. But by the time I was born, we had perfectly good leather and chainmail armor. We had just as good leatherworkers and smiths as any other people, thank you. And when we were victorious, the tradition of those times was to take the mail off the dead on the battlefield, so we had plenty of foreign-worked armor, as well."

"So...you *never* fought naked?" I had to admit I was disappointed.

He grinned at me. "Enjoying the mental picture, eh? But that would be like me saying to you, 'Oh, so you Yanks fight in breeches with muskets.' We had hundreds of years of Pictland. Do you think we did not evolve in all that time? But it is also *not inaccurate* to say that my ancestors did *sometimes* pull off their tunics for fighting."

"Why would they do that?"

"Well...the historians have guessed *somewhat* right, there. Our tattoos gave us power and protection in battle. They were spells in our skin. *And* they were intimidating. As well, to tear off your clothing expresses a complete disdain for your opponent. It is both an insult and a threat. And to back that up, once our warriors would strip down, they would then scream more insults and threats at the enemy, perform feats of strength in front of them. Still naked. Try to imagine *that*. And then that same naked tattooed man leading a charge of men running at you, their battle-cries filling the air. It scared the piss out of our enemies. *Literally*."

Wulfhram huffed, "And they called us *berserkr!*"

"Yes. And I'm sorry you have to deal with that being trendy with the kee, now. I can only imagine how annoying it is. We have not spoken of this in some time, but you may recall my people had the same battle-madness, which we called the *miri-cath*. Our greatest warriors had it, and you could say it was the *miri-cath* that inspired them to strip naked and do feats of strength, and run screaming at the enemy, one man to slaughter many."

"Maybe the kee will discover this and start making foolish TV shows about your peoples instead of mine."

"Why d'you think I keep messing with archeologists? If they know nothing about my people, they cannot make History Channel specials about us. Or worse, *historical fiction*."

"Do you actively destroy artifacts?" I was horrified at the thought.

"Oh, I have not. Well, some things have gone missing before they could be displayed in museums. But the damp conditions of my land mean that there is not much I need to do: metal rusts to nothing, and leather and linen melt into mud. They can't do much with a few carved stones. But if I wanted to *help*, there are hoards I could unearth, all sorts of hidden things I could bring to kee daylight. But I would rather be out in that daylight with no sunglasses, thank you, than to give the kee any knowledge of my people.

"But again I find I have interrupted the story. Please continue, *mo faol-chù*."

"It is fine. You gave me time to remember. It started as a very bad day for us. I was not the only one who drank deep of ale the night before. And that beach was made of little stones, not nice soft sand. But if you drink enough, you do not notice! So we were not up at the break of dawn, and we had only started rousing ourselves when the first arrows rained down on us—not a very nice way to wake up!

"It was not a warm night, and we were all accustomed to sleeping in our clothes and boots. So once we realized what was going on, those near their shields held them up, and the rest of us pulled on our mail shirts and helmets in safety, then took the shields to return the favor. But while I was holding that shield, I have this memory of a man I liked—for some reason I still remember his name, Leif

Tokeson—staring with one dead eye at me, a Pictish arrow sticking out from the other.

"Of course I had seen death many times before that, both given to those I was fighting and those who fought beside me. I do not know why that moment stays in my mind. Perhaps because it was the start of the day when everything changed.

"It only took me a few moments to get on my mail shirt and helmet. Then I grabbed my own shield and held it next to the man who had been protecting me, and together we protected more men as they prepared to do battle. My uncle was shouting orders to his men, and we were glad to follow them because it brought order to the chaos. The other lords were doing the same, and soon we made three *skjaldborg*, about fifty men each, ready to use our spears and battleaxes and swords. I started with a spear that I grabbed from near me, but my sword Mjǫtuðr is never far from my side."

Wulfhram caressed the sword at his side. "Is that the same sword, after all these years?" I asked, having already lost a beloved blade in a cave in the bottom of the world. Being an am'r can be hard on weapons.

"No. The first Mjǫtuðr—this means "Dispenser of Fate"—was stolen when I died the mortal death. But I have faithfully recreated her—more than once—and her spirit lives on in each blade.

"And she was right here at my side on that fateful day. Ah! You two, do not give each other that look; I am *not* being full of drama! My peoples understood fate, *ørlǫg*, as a most important force in one's life. That day I met my fate, and that is *why* I am here telling you—trying to tell you—my story, and not food for the ravens and the worms long since.

"I worshiped Thor as my main god when I was kee, but since I became am'r I know I have become one of Odin's: that the twisty-minded oath-breaker is the one I must sacrifice to if I don't want to be left alone in the indifferent hands of the Norns.

"But I did not know any of this was to come, that day. I checked that Mjǫtuðr was safe at my side, grabbed a spear, and overlapped my shield with the shield being held up by the man beside me, and then the next fighter overlapped their shield upon mine.

"When we had organized as rapidly as possible into three shield walls, five fighters deep, we began drumming the shields. We all began to feel more secure. Today you'd call it the "comfort zone." I had been in the *skjaldborg* so many times by then. I knew the fighters to either side of me, knew their strengths and weaknesses, and which ones I could count on.

"Arrows thunked into my shield and stuck there, but did not prevent our shield wall from growing. The fire-arrows *were* an issue, for our shields were wood, oiled to keep from getting waterlogged. They were *not* fireproof. The fire was easily enough put out—but to do so you had to take your shield out of the wall. That made a weak place that the enemy could exploit. The Picts ran out of fire-arrows soon enough. The main force of them had lined up to fight us, and we started telling them what cowards they had been, first hiding in the trees and letting archers do their work instead of coming out to fight like men, and now that they were here, they were too likely to get scared and run away, and they *should* be scared; here we cried out the names of our most renowned warriors, with a deed they had done—"

"Like what? What kind of things did you say?"

"Oh, like, 'I am Leif Leifson, who killed Æthelgeat the Mighty, who had slain twenty men before I chopped him down like a tree with this axe right here, called Skull-Splitter.' We said the same lines in each battle. Battle-poetry, you could say, recited both to frighten the enemy and to make our own adrenaline pump harder."

"Of course, we had to shout loud, to be heard over the maniacs across from us. They were shouting much the same things. And they did not all stay in their line, but some ran out into the space between and did stunts. We mocked them. They dared us to break the *skjaldborg* and meet us for single combat. We knew not to give in to their jibes; we held the wall strong."

"Did, um, any strip down naked?" I could feel Dubhghall glaring at me.

"Ha! No, I am sad to let you down. None stripped naked, although some had bare arms with tattoos showing on them. They carried these tiny little round shields, which to me seemed worse than useless. Why carry such a pathetic shield? To carry another sword would give more protection! I had gone a-Víking in this area, but mostly monasteries and surprise raids on villages, so I had not faced a force of armed Pictish warriors before. They had spears like ours, but their swords were shorter and their shields so itty-bitty. They seemed like little terrier-dogs, barking at our heels.

"And when we finally met them in battle, I found the comparison not wrong. They did not meet our shield wall with shield wall—they could not, not with those round bucklers—but they did a far more intelligent thing. They met our shield wall with a spear wall.

"A *skjaldborg* can a powerful thing, it can be a thing that terrifies your enemies. But part of its power is its reputation. Men know that a *skjaldborg* is deadly, and so they die before it. But there are things that break a *skjaldborg*. The *svinfylking*, a fighting wedge, is the most well-known method. But simply meeting a shield wall with a spear wall will do it, too.

"We had the best formation we could muster after the confusion of waking up to fire-arrows, the result of the many years of battle experience held by our leaders and many of our fighters. If we had been fighting another *skjaldborg,* the odds would have been on us; we were fueled with the desperation of hearing our ships burning behind us. But we were not a wall of shields facing a wall of shields. Instead, we faced a long wall of bristling spears, aimed with determination at our every weak spot. We called the spear 'mail-piercer' for good reason.

"Death in a *skjaldborg*-meeting-a-*skjaldborg* is up-close work. Your shield slams against your enemy's shield, and you look them in the eye, you hear their breathing and groaning, you smell their sweat and blood and their piss as well. Your short sword, the *seax,* is your best weapon, jabbing between the shields through chainmail and leather to bury into guts. Or putting out those eyes that stare hatred into yours. Either way, it is confined, cramped, intimate death.

"But a spear is two to three meters long and—"

"I'm sorry," I hated to stop his flow, and particularly for this embarrassing reason. "What's that in feet? I still kinda think in American units..."

"Hmmmm? Ah, not to worry. The Romans used feet as well, and they took over the world. In feet...six to ten feet. It is a very different kind of fighting, at such a distance. You can kill your enemy before you see their face, if their helm has cheek plates. You do not feel them die as you would on your sword; just thrust and if you aim right they drop, and if they do not drop you thrust again. Unless your spear gets stuck or broken, but that is another matter.

"We tried to cover our dismay by beating our swords harder on our shields, and our leaders led us in chants of how we would kill them all. And then it was the moment when we started walking towards them, and they started walking towards us. In the *skjaldborg*, we needed to keep our shield matched with the shields on either side, and so we walked in a slow rhythm to meet our fame or to meet our deaths.

"The spear wall did not need the same constraints, but the Picts wanted to do the most damage possible, and the way to do that was simply holding a formation so that the mass of their spears hit us at the same moment, making thinking impossible from that point, only reaction."

"Um. I'm sorry to interrupt. But didn't you have any spears?"

"*Nei, nei,* it is good question! Yes, we did. But in the shield wall, spears are used by the fighters in the second row. The ones at the front hold the shields, and it is a real responsibility. I cannot impress upon you enough how vital it is to keep the wall. The ones behind may have shields as well, to hold above the fighters in the front in case of arrows, or they may have spears, which can come out above or between the shields. This is very effective against another *skjaldborg*, as you can imagine. But against a spear wall, it is nothing. And we did not have enough spears to make our own spear wall. But we did have battleaxes: the *Skeggøx*, the "bearded axe" which has a hook that extends below the edge, making a wide cutting surface. Our swords could not counter a spear, but a good sweep of the *Skeggøx* could tug a weapon or shield out of our enemies grasp. We just needed to get close enough, and our bearded axes would smash the deadly mail-piercers or yank them out of unwilling hands.

"When we met, there was death. And at first, it was all ours. The hewing-spears hit shields and it made us stop, for when one of us was stopped in their tracks, so the rest of us had to stay with them, to keep the integrity of the wall. But some of the spears hit legs not protected by shields. And some spears broke through the shields and found the bodies behind them. I could hear screams around me from the ones who had been found by the spears. It was hot and sweaty in the *skjaldborg*, and it felt like each panting one of us was making the space more stifling. But I needed each panting one of us to keep their shield *right where it was*—I had almost no freedom of movement with which to protect myself from those incessant spearheads, but in that lack of freedom was our shared protection, our shared hope of vengeance. I would not let down the ones beside me, and I prayed to Thor they would not let me down.

"My Lord Áleifr screamed at us to keep moving. We took a step forward together. Spears crashed against shields, spears crashed through shields, spears destroyed the knees and calves of those along the line. Fighters moved up to take the place of fallen ones. We took a step forward together. Those hewing-spears battered us. We took another step forward together towards our desperate goal, for if we could close up with the Picts, their spears became useless, and they would have to either retreat from us or drop their spears and use their little swords and their little shields. So we fought grimly forward towards our advantage, towards a place where we could give some repayment for the fighters we lost with each step.

"We never got there. I called them terrier-dogs before, and that is what they were like. Little Pict warriors ran out from behind their spear wall, and came at us on either flank, nipping at our heels and distracting us.

"And we were distracted already, dealing with this spear wall. We had our fighters in three walls, ten men across, five deep. Their spear wall stretched out at least fifty fighters across. It was a thin wall, but for too long they were not taking enough damage for it to matter. That long wall began to curl around us, and on our right and left flanks, fighters were ordered to break from the *skjaldborg* and attack both their harriers and that dangerously engulfing spear wall.

"I was in the center wall, which was still unbroken. Áleifr screamed orders again. The remaining shield walls all stopped their slow forward progress and we advanced as fast as a *skjaldborg* can go and maintain integrity. It was vital that we break this spear wall, or we would all die on this beach with our ships burning down into the waves behind us.

"It was the only plan that would do any good. It did *some* good. We brought the fight to the Picts, and I got the satisfaction of getting in under those mail-piercers, finally wetting my sword with Pictish blood. We got close enough that I was using even my shield as a weapon, slamming their little bodies away as if they were children.

"But at this point their spear wall and our shield walls unraveled like skeins of yarn. They no longer had an advantage from it, and for us, the frustration of this whole disastrous battle took its toll and our discipline dissolved once we started our share of the killing.

"Again, I found myself dealing with frustrating little terriers. They should have been at a huge disadvantage through their smaller size and lesser shielding and armor. But they seemed to have no idea of this. They fought independently—although they could work together and Thor-help-you if you found two of them going at you. They were game; they ran at us with no evident fear. They were tenacious as Hel and didn't seem to notice injuries short of losing a limb. They had far too much energy. And the lack of heavy shields and armor meant they were very quick. And they fought smart; if you didn't pay close attention, they would get in under your shield and have you hamstrung in a second. They closed in around the sides of our shield walls and nipped our heels from behind; our shield walls disintegrated.

"It was the most frustrating battle of my life. These little hellhounds—blood-stained guardians of Hel's gate—made fools of us. You would think you had one bleeding and exhausted, and then he would nip in and slice the tendons at the front of your elbow, and your sword would fall from your hand, and he would nip in again and stab you in the neck or the side, and you would be bleeding out and unable to hold onto your sword so you could go to Valhalla.

"Obviously, this did not happen to me, but I saw it happening all around me. Battle is always violent chaos, but this was the most unpredictable, uncontrollable battle I'd experienced. The best part of the battle is figuring the enemy out and forcing him to do what you want him to do, either as a group or one-on-one. There was no figuring these mad little creatures out, you just had to try and kill them quick, using superior strength and reach, and then be ready for the next one to be throwing himself upon you, screaming incomprehensible battle cries and jabbing those little swords anywhere and everywhere.

"At first I was just aggravated, infuriated. I couldn't get the battle-glory to flow through me, because it was all just a headache. But after a few Pictish swords stung deep enough, my anger changed and grew and became what I needed. I began to dance with my little enemies, to see their patterns and anticipate them—and then end them. It was exhilarating, and I loved my little foes for as long as they lasted, and I thanked them for their challenge, for their bold madness and pluck and wit, for their refusal to die until I had killed them each three times over.

"It was hot on that beach, with the heat of the burning ships behind us. I was tired, probably hungover, and completely what we would call 'dehydrated' these days. I had smashed down my shield onto a little terrier who was frustrating me, and it had cracked as it broke his skull and slammed down into his spine. All I needed was this, was me and my Mjǫtuðr, who flowed around me like a melody over the throbbing song of violence around us.

"As the combat climaxed—Why are you both snickering? Is that a wrong word?—two of the little hellhounds ran at me, and for a while we danced together. Both were agile and when I blocked one, the other's blows would land. Perhaps these little folk never slept, just spent their tiny lives fighting from the second they were born until someone finally stopped their sword arms for good. That seemed possible, at this point in time. They danced around me and I was full of the battle glory so I no longer felt thirsty or hot or tired; I was just focused on killing this next little hellhound so I could kill the next one after him as well. They were trying for killing shots to my body, and my mail was holding them off so far, but I was getting sore, and I knew that my mail would eventually fail under a future cut. I lost patience with the dance. I finished off the one on my right with an unexpected spin and a sweeping blow which took off his little hellhound head.

"That just left the other. I had apparently killed his brother or his friend, for he rushed at me and yelled into my face words I did not know but could easily understand. He called me a beast he would slaughter, a giant he would slay, and he said I had no intelligence, only muscles. Some ideas can cross a language barrier: love and hate both do it best.

"'I am Wulfhram,' I replied to him, 'I killed your friend and now I will be your death this day, *køuærne*, little dog.'

"I followed these words with a cleaving strike, as I had done with the other one, a sweeping full-arm movement intended to take his head off his diminutive body and be done with it.

"But the hellhound rolled under the blow. He switched his replying blow to an offhand strike that glanced off my thigh, just below where my mail ended, and hard enough to slice into the muscle. The sting of it broke into my battle madness and focused me even more tightly on finishing him.

"I drew back the bleeding leg, and raised my sword up high, pivoting the sword offside to get a slower, more controlled cut, down onto where his neck met his shoulder. It *should* have been a killing stroke.

"But the little terrier had his sword up in time to block the powerful blow. It drove him to his knees, but his neck was still all too undamaged for me. Irritated by his agility, I kicked his chest and knocked him back onto the little rocks of the beach.

"He should have had the wind knocked out of him—when I kick a man he normally *stays down*—but this little hellhound rolled to the left, and as I brought down what should have been the killing stroke *this time*, he slashed his little sword upward across my sword-arm's shoulder, cutting through mail and leather. It was more than an irritation—this kind of injury would slow me down soon enough.

"And he brought his arm around again for another slash! I was *done* with this unteachable puppy. I lifted my arm—despite the pain that arced down it and down my back—and slammed the pommel of my sword into his face. He fell back. The blow had not landed on his nose, as I had hoped, which would have shoved it back into his brain. It just gashed open his forehead. Blood gushed down the sides of his head, poured down into his eyes. He was blinded by it, and he should have been concussed as well.

"I dropped to my knees to finally send this hell-pup back where he'd come from. Perhaps the wound on my shoulder was sapping my strength, perhaps I had lost more blood than I realized. All I could think was that I just wanted to get him within my reach and make sure the job was finished. As I used my plummeting bodyweight to put momentum into my final—*this time!*—blow, the tricky little terrier had one final bite for me. He angled his sword up. It was just a movement of a wrist, using the ground beneath to stabilize his sword. As I plunged down upon him, I found I had also plunged myself down upon his sword. My sword found his neck, at last! But all I could do was fall further onto his blade, onto his body, islanding the smooth little stones of the beach as the red river of our mingling blood ran down to meet the ocean.

"And that is the last I remember, until I woke up in a very different place."

Wulfhram sat back. The way he settled back into his seat made it clear he was done speaking. If he were kee I'd offer him a drink at this point, something boozy. But being am'r made that offer awkward at best—I didn't have a kee on hand to offer up. And I still was not comfortable with classifying sentient beings as walking juice boxes. And then, the fact that am'r preferred "vhoon-vaa"—*playing* with their dinner, wink wink, nudge nudge—added to that *not* being an option available to me in the moment. Being a good hostess in the am'r world was a complication I'd not come anywhere close to figuring out. And an *ethical* version of that was entirely beyond me, at least for now.

Dubhghall and I took a moment to give Wulfhram the best applause: appreciative silence. Then Dubhghall took over the narrative.

"That is not *precisely* how I remember it, although to be fair I probably was indeed a hell-pup that day. Once the battle had properly kicked off, I took the terror that threatened to turn my bowels liquid and worked it out by attacking every Northman I could.

"I remember seeing *this* wee great walloper and deciding he'd do just fine. And he is right: I *was* with my friend, one whom I'd grown up with and trained with, Uurgust. He'd come with me when the King raised the men; we had drunk until vomiting that night. We had ridden our hill-ponies side by side the next day and covered our fear with moans of drink-sickness. He had stood beside me in the wood, and marched out beside me, our spears in hand, to meet the *schiltron.*

"It is strange. I'd almost forgotten him. When I think back to that day, I remember myself as a lone warrior. And I suppose each warrior must face battle alone, must face their fear alone no matter how many stand beside them. And then...the rest of my memories are what has taken over. I left Uurgust a headless rotting corpse on the beach without a second thought, caught up in the strangeness of all that was to come."

Dubhghall closed his eyes, and I watched emotion wash through him. Whatever he was about to tell, whatever it was that was so intense it had made him forget his old friend for centuries, was paused for a moment to not just grieve the death of a friend, but to fully acknowledge the shame of having treated that friend so inadequately in memory.

Then he let out a deep breath. He opened his black eyes to meet mine, and I almost recoiled from the roil of emotion in them. But he spoke as lightly as ever.

"As I think you know, am'r are as called to a battlefield as ravens; both feed there. And to that battlefield, at that moment, came the am'r who would change both our lives forever.

"His name was Zigor."

I responded before I could remind myself I was just supposed to listen, "Was it *really?*"

Dubhghall snorted. "I know, I know. It sounds like a bad guy from a bad fantasy movie. But it really was his name. He was originally of the *euskaldunak* people, and they have names like that. But I am getting ahead of myself.

"I was lying there dying of blood loss, and it was a death made worse for being crushed under that outsize blond bawbag there, who was sprawled unconscious, dying atop me.

"I don't remember anything after that; it all went black at some point. But then, an infinity or an instant later, I felt a brutal pain in my neck. I'd enough mind left to realize my blood was being drunk, and I remember thinking something like, "Gae on, take those last wee drops, it's not enough to feed man or beast." But then, to my amaze-ment, there was hot blood spilling onto my lips, and my mouth was forced open, and I could either choke or swal-low. Clearly, I did the latter. And then the darkness over-came me again, and I knew nothing."

"It was the same for me," Wulfhram threw in. "Except that I do not remember being drunk from. I was so very close to the shield-roofed feasting hall of Valhalla! But then the blood pulled me back into my body. I was angry!"

"I came round hearing that argument," Dubhghall laughed, "and thank the gods I knew the language of the Northmen, or we might not be sitting here talking to you now. This pure giant gowk I'd thought I'd killed was shout-ing—*weakly* mind you—at this other man, dressed in mail and splattered in mud and blood and worse, like the rest of us. And *he's* laughing and arguing back. I'll try and do it jus-tice..." Here he cleared his throat, and imitated Wulfhram's deeper voice and phrasing.

"'I deserved a warrior's reward! How dare you take that from me?!'

And then, in another voice, light and sardonic: "'Do not worry. I have given you a greater reward: a body forever youthful, a sword-arm strengthened, a strategist's mind sharpened, an endless blood lust. Your Valhalla is here on earth. This is what I am giving you.'

"'What is this nonsense? Will I feast with Odin and his shieldmaidens every night, and rise every morning to fight the bravest warriors all over again? No. You have taken that from me, and I will be avenged!'

"'Do not be tiresome. If I had let you die you would not have found any of that. You would just have been food for the ravens, a corpse alive only with maggots. I am giving you the only true eternity a person can know.'

"Before the muckle gowk—that's 'big fool'—of a Northman could attempt to get up and make the fight physical, I asked the stranger, 'Could you explain this for those of us who were *not* expecting to go to Odin's Mead Hall?'

"'Ahhh, not just a fierce warrior, but one with a brain, as well.' The Muckle Northman growled at this, but the stranger continued, 'Yes. There is a special tribe of people, and there is only one way to become part of them. I have started the process with you *both* because I could not let such powerful fighters go to waste. Normally, we am'r—that is our name for our tribe—make only one new one at a time. But I could not choose between you—I must have you both!'

"I did not like the sound of that. Muckle Northman did not either, I could tell by how his body stiffened. 'How is it that you *have us*, precisely?'

"'Oh, take no offense. You are neither a captive nor slave. I will do a blood ritual with you two more times. That will ensure your transformation to am'r. You will become stronger than ever before, a greater warrior than you ever could have hoped to be in your life. Then, in exchange for my gifts to you, you will spend a while with me, traveling the world to the greatest battles, fighting the fiercest foes in places far beyond your imagining.'

"'How is that our repayment to you?'

"'Quick-Minded One! You shall be a joy to me. While you stay with me, we will continue our blood rituals. Your blood in that time will be especially powerful to me. Indeed, it will enrich us both, and each ritual will make us greater.

"'But that state is transitory. You will not fully be as strong as I, not while you live as you do now. Eventually, in some future battle you will receive what to a normal man would be a killing blow. I will bury you with loving care—and you shall rise as a full am'r, with all the strengths of our tribe.'

"'You say we are *not* your slaves, but you have not mentioned us having any *choice* in this.' Muckle Northman stirred at my words, but I glared at him to keep quiet.

"'See yourselves as sworn liegemen. The oath comes with the blood ritual. In time, you will be lords amongst the am'r as well.'

"Muckle Northman had had enough. 'I will not accept you as my liege! I do not know you, and I do not like you! Unless I have a choice of my lord, then I am a slave! I will not be a slave!'

"The stranger looked annoyed, 'Look, I have saved you from imminent death. I offer you all the power you ever dreamt of. I offer you an eternity of that power. Is this not enough for you to return to me some good will?'

"Muckle Northman was clinging to his main point. '*I will not be a slave!*' he roared with impressive reserves of hidden strength.

"I thought this a good moment to interject myself. 'Sir—understand; all you say is very new to us. I have never heard of any *am'r*, and clearly neither has my friend here. We are having trouble coming to terms with what you must admit is a major change in our circumstances.'

"The stranger seemed somewhat mollified, so I rolled on, 'And we both nearly died recently, so neither of us are at our best.'

"'I will fix that'—he glared at Muckle Northman—'if you will let me. The next blood ritual will strengthen your body and your mind. And it is not...unenjoyable.'

"We all paused. I wanted time to think: the stranger was pressing us too hard. Certainly too hard for Muckle Northman. I thought he would try to murder the stranger at any second, with probable bad results for all of us. But he surprised me.

"'Are these am'r...are they *berserkr?*"

"The stranger brightened. 'An excellent question! You dig to the heart of it! The little dark one does not have all the brains, I see! Yes, we *are*. The true berserkers. And I chose you both because I witnessed your fight. I saw the battle madness in you'—he turned to me—'and what you would call the *miri-cath*. You were transcendent, raised above the other fighters by the poetry of war.

"'I shall never forget your fight together! And that is what led us all here, now.' He spread his hands and gestured. I had been so focused on the two other men—and the bizarre circumstances—that I'd not noticed our surroundings. There was not much to notice. We must be in one of the caves in a large cave system along the coastline. A fire in the center between us brought much needed warmth and light. Muckle Northman did not look his best: alive, but had clearly been near death. Overly wan skin was stretched tight across his face; dark hollows circled his eyes.

"I felt like he looked.

"The stranger, however, almost glowed with vigor. His skin was plump with youth. He was dark-haired, his skin was a cool shade of tan. He had a harsh wedge of a nose, like an axe-blade, and his brown-black eyes seemed always to be squinting into some too-bright sun.

"Meanwhile, Muckle Northman had been having a wee think. 'So, you are an *yfir-berserkr*? I have seen ones like you in battle. Not just men who have worked themselves up into a frenzy or drunk the madness drug. Men who have the Battle Gods inside them, flowing through their veins. *That* is what you offer me?'

"'You understand now! Yes, *that* is what I offer you, the path to that power and glory. And you will not mind walking that path, I promise you...'

"Muckle Northman didn't need convincing. 'I would be a true berserker. What must I do?'"

Wulfhram jumped into Dubhghall's recreated dialogue, "*Bíddu!* Wait! I do not think I was so easily convinced! I argued more. I am no fool, to be so easily swayed by pretty words."

"Apologies, *mo faol-chù.* Yes, I'm sure you were far more tenacious—*mulish,* even—in not giving any personal rights away, and in fully understanding (as best any kee can understand the am'r existence) what Zigor was offering us. Well, what he had started giving us without asking, and then was belatedly trying to talk us into. I am turning truth into tale. Noosh, here, does not need every syllable we uttered, just the basic gist."

"Make sure the basic gist is not making me look like a *fífl* and you a wise hero."

"Would I do that to you, *mo faol-chù?*" Wulfhram did not look entirely convinced, and Dubhghall hurried on, "Well, anyway, you saved us from things being more unpleasant than they might have been. I was not particularly convinced by this egotistical stranger, but once you determined that the powers of the berserker, of the *miri-cath*, would be bestowed upon us, you accepted the inevitable, which encouraged me to accept it as well.

"I think if we had not given consent, Zigor might have just drained us both dry, using our bodies as he chose in our weakened states, and you would not have gone to Valhalla, nor I to reside with my ancestors. We would have just rotted, alone together, in that cave, and some archaeologist would have found our bones and completely made a hash of the guessing what we were doing there. So, *mo faol-chù*, you saved my life. It is no small thing."

"Well, you have saved me from being given my tokhmarenc many times since then, so we are more than even, *litilmenni*."

"I think Noosh would like more of the story, instead of our bickering."

I did not tell them that I could have listened to them "bicker" for hours. They had been moving through this world together for so long that they could finish each other's sentences, especially the insults.

Wulfhram nodded and held out an open palm in agreement.

Dubhghall continued, "What was I saying? Ah, there we were in the cave, sitting around the fire, with a man we still thought of as a disturbing stranger. None of us yet knew each other's names. But once Wulfhram had become positive about the blood ritual idea, that changed everything."

"You were not, uh, freaked out by the idea of doing a blood ritual with this disturbing stranger?"

"Ah. You modern folk. For me, the idea of a blood ritual was nothing shocking. In the most mundane parts of our lives, we ingested animal blood. You have heard of black pudding? This comes from our idea of 'fast food' at this time. A Pictish warband had to travel light, whether we were escaping from a cattle raid on our neighbors or a skirmish with an external enemy. We warriors all carried a bag of oats. And we brought with us a bullock or two—meals on the hoof, as it were. When we needed food, we wasted no part of the cattle. We boiled its flesh in a cooking pot made of its skin. And we'd bled it, first, and mixed that blood with our oats for nutritious cakes we cooked on hot stones from the fire. With some wild herbs, they are delicious; I wish I could still eat them.

"But that is just the start of what we did with blood. For we had a ceremony to tie people together, what you might today call 'blood brothers,' but done by a priest, with magic to deepen the blood bond. In this ceremony, the two who were building that connection drank each other's blood, right from the vein. It was a solemn, beautiful thing.

"So the idea of a blood ritual did not 'freak me out.' The idea of exchanging blood with a stranger who I did not particularly *like* was less comfortable. But even then, it could hurt only on a *spiritual* level—we certainly had no concept of blood-born illnesses at that time.

"To be honest, I figured, at worst, we'd do some weird blood ritual with this weird stranger—no harm done—and then once we both had recovered some strength, we could kill him easily—two against one—and then go our separate ways."

I laughed. "Being honest as well—that's kinda how I felt when I went home with Sandu the first night. Well, I didn't think I could *kill* him. But I really didn't buy into his story right away. It was too damn implausible. But I thought: well, have a night of fun, probably no harm done."

Wulfhram howled with laughter and Dubhghall grinned hugely and said, "Oh, Noosh, you have given us a gift. We've seen that bastard in high moods and low, despairing and victorious...but the thought of the Voivode Vlad Țepeș *him-*

self bringing home a kee girl who is just *humoring the weirdo*, and having to prove himself, after all these centuries of lording it over us all...Oh! It is too good!"

Wulfhram had subsided into chuckling. It filled me with warm pleasure to hear my lover (who could indeed be too full of himself) roasted by friends who knew him well.

But it made me think. "You two are both older than Sandu, by like, five hundred years. Does it bother you that he is treated as more—I don't know—treated with more respect than you?"

Wulfhram was instantly serious. "There is no less respect. If any am'r does not show me proper respect, he does not live much longer."

"Indeed," Dubhghall added, "Dae nae worry aboot us, lass. Neither this *faol-chù* nor I have any issues with a lack of deference from other am'r."

"But, but, if Bagamil ever gets given his tokhmarenc, wouldn't Sandu become the default head of the am'r?"

"It is true Bagamil is the eldest of the am'r and is accorded respect as Aojysht-of-aojyshtaish on that level. But Sandu has the vhoon-anghyaa of Bagamil directly, not many lives removed, as the rest of us do. *You* have the same bloodline—as do few am'r still alive today. The vhoon you get from your patar is not a small matter; it shapes you as genes do for the kee. Sandu may be younger than Wulfhram and I in years, but *strength* is the most important aspect in the am'r world. We recognize Sandu's puissance. He, nonetheless, has always shown the both of us deepest respect. As well as friendship. You know that in the world of the am'r, trust and trustworthiness is the rarest gift. And misplaced trust the most frequent cause of receiving your tokhmarenc."

"No," Wulfhram corrected, "Being a damn fool is."

"You are right, *mo bhràthair*. And, Noosh, the vhoon-anghyaa we received from Zigor was not useless. Over time, we found out that he was truly a mighty warrior. He was perhaps a little single-minded in that focus, but as both this Muckle Northman and I were similarly minded in those days, it was not a mismatch for a patar and his frithaputhraish.

"Not that we learned those terms right away: the maker of an am'r and the ones being made into am'r. Zigor was never much of a teacher. He did what he wanted, and you either learned from him or you did not. He was not stupid and he would answer questions, if you figured out the right things to ask, and you got him in the right mood, which was usually when he was mellow after vhoon-vaa. Or sharpening his weapons: that always made him contemplative.

"But first I must tell you how things worked out in that cave. He'd dragged us in there as the sun was setting, so

we still had the rest of the night, after his pitch had finally landed right with us. It was the most informal "blood
ritual" I'd ever seen—certainly no druid priest leading the
ceremony! But then, when Wulfhram and I discovered the
aphrodisiac effects of vhoon (which we had missed the first
time on account of being mostly dead), we were glad for
the lack of priests, who'd certainly have ruined the mood.
Any priest I've ever known was into shit far too kinky for my
comfort!

"I can see you trying not to ask, which is polite but unnec-
essary. Yes, we had sex with Zigor, and while experiencing
the vhoon-intoxication we all three explored all the ways in
which male bodies can experience pleasure together. Once
the vhoon had taken hold, it was no longer a matter of
the fact that I was with an enemy and a dubious stranger,
whose names I did not even know. It was now simply about
vhoon, about not letting these incredible sensations come
to an end.

"And now you'll be wanting to know, was it my first time
with a man? The modern world is so *fixated* with things
like this. The time I am from, this was simply a non-is-
sue. We warrior-lads enjoyed 'winching' certainly, but we
just as happily took warmth and pleasure in each other's
bodies, when no women were around, and some of us preferred that. Certainly, there was experimentation in the

randy hormonal years, with only the increasing influence of the Roman Church over our more tolerant Christianity, *Crìosdaidheachd*, causing there to be negative connotations around the love between men. When I was growing up, to deeply love another man was as masculine as you could get. Today, it is only 'manly' to kill another man, not love him."

Wulfhram spoke up. "It was not much different with us. As men, we were expected to take wives and have babies; it was a commitment to pass on our name into future generations. But that was not about *love*. As long as your name was passed on, and as long as you did not interfere with another man's household, who you also loved was of no concern. Indeed, our sagas are full of both gay ribaldry and love stories. And the Gods! They let nothing so trivial as gender get in the way of their lusts!"

"You see, there was no reason for any of us to feel any shame in that cave, or in any of the days and nights following that one. It was an unusual start for Wulfhram and me, us coming from the kee world where we were mortal enemies. But once we had entered the world of the am'r, old prejudices fell away. I soon knew *mo faol-chù* as I knew few men. We neither of us knew Zigor very well, except perhaps to judge his moods, but we certainly knew what he enjoyed in bed."

"Uh, actually, I was going to ask about something else. But it was, uh, fascinating to learn all that."

I swear, Dubhghall was as close to blushing as an am'r over a thousand years old could be. "What," he asked dryly, "were you wanting to ask, then?"

"You said before you were Christian, but then you talked about Druid priests. I didn't think Christianity allowed for believing in more than one religion at a time...?"

"Ah, you only know the intolerant sects of the modern day. In my time and place, we had a form of Christianity which had incorporated many of our older beliefs and practices. For some centuries, while the Druidic faith as a whole had been replaced, there were many commonalities with Christian bishops, priests, deacons—and especially the hermits—who took over many of the roles that the druids had performed. You can perhaps tell this by how many "saints" we had; take a few steps and you'd trip over one! Many of our traditions were kept safe by this syncretization for centuries, although by my time, those blood rituals were seldom done by priests...but before a battle or other vital moment, things could get a good deal more 'pagan' and no one looked askance. But we have lost the story!

"Zigor had found a good cave, dry and deep. We had no reason to leave in the days it took to do our 'blood ritual' fully three times. And then some for good measure—we worked well together. It was not until we left that we fully realized how great were the changes rendered in our flesh. I'd never noticed that after some point, no one had bothered to make a fire again, for we neither needed the light nor the heat. I can tell you the first sunrise I encountered was a *nasty* shock—and smoked glass spectacles were still many years in the future."

"What did you do without them?" I shuddered to think of am'r life without my security-blankie shades.

"We avoided daylight as much as possible. Zigor was particularly ill-tempered with a sun-migraine. Unfortunately, many battles are fought during the day. When we had to fight under the too-bright sun, we would all try and channel our pain into pain for our opponents. In the heat of battle, you can forget a headache.

"What Zigor had promised us was not a lie. Wulfhram and I had indeed reached new heights as warriors, and when the battle madness was upon us, we left food for the ravens each way we turned—even as mere am'r-nafsh, even before we became full am'r and attained our full strength.

"We three formed a mercenary band that was soon referred to as if we were from legend and myth. Desperate rulers would beg us to help defend their kingdoms. Alternatively, if we showed up in an area, suspicious rulers would send their most famed fighters to ambush us, or even set assassins upon us. Either way, we had fun, and honed our skills sharper upon the best warriors the world had to offer us.

"Besides the promised strength and power, Zigor delivered a life I could never have dreamt of, back in the days of cattle-raiding and wenching. Almost all of the warrior-lads I'd practiced with would never in their life leave, say, a fifty-kilometer radius from their homes. If I hadn't fought Wulfhram, if Zigor had not made us his frithaputhraish, I would have skirmished with my neighbors, and with Northman and Celt and Saxon and Dane. I would've married, and run my father's lands, and contributed to the long line of *Mac Dhùgaill*..." He stopped, with a faraway look. "I find our clan has since moved to the west of where my family lived. Perhaps if I'd stayed in the kee world, that would be different today...I do still keep my eye on them, who would have been my descendants. Anyways...eventually, one of those skirmishes would have given me a wound our healers could not heal, or a plague would have come along, or some other kee mortality. I might have died of some *mishap*, like slipping and hitting my head! I have thought often on it, but I truly have no regrets on leaving that life behind.

"But, speaking of regrets, and of that final battle, well, my life as it is now does still have them. Regret, that is. Wulfhram and I haven't escaped that as am'r—perhaps we've tasted it *more*, in the centuries we've survived.

"As I said, we got to explore much more of the world than most who lived in the Ninth Century. When the Northmen used their boats for trading—and reconnaissance—instead of raiding, we would catch rides with them. Wulfhram of course was useful in this regard, because as good as my Norsk was, his was obviously better. But Zigor was a true polyglot—as well as having a strength for mesmerizing kee, which we both appreciate coming down to us in our vhoon-anghyaa. So upon any vessel big enough to hold us all, we would find a place. We traveled across Frankia—plenty of fighting there! Zigor was always determined to avoid Al-Andalus, so we traveled through Beneventum, and then there was more than plenty for us to do on the *clusterbùrach* which was the Italian peninsula. We crossed over to Africa and fought our way through the Rustamid Imamate of Tahert, what was left of the Byzantine territories, and the Abbasid Caliphate. Then we moved back up into the Roman Empire—now in the east!—and when we got bored there, up into Bulgaria, which was a lot bigger back then."

"We were there before Sandu was! Ha!" Wulfhram beamed.

"Wallachia was part of the First Bulgarian Empire," Dubhghall explained. "And this wee dunderclunk never tires of reminding your man that we were there *first*. It's funny—I have no idea where Bagamil was at this time; I've never thought to ask."

"We know Bagamil was not in the area because *he* was near there," Wulfhram growled, his mood suddenly dark, "And *he* always stayed far away from Bagamil. A coward! But a smart coward!"

"Wait, huh, who?" This had gone in a direction I was not expecting.

"You are getting ahead of the story," Dubhghall admonished Wulfhram. He turned back to me, "So as I was saying, we were in Bulgaria. From there, a delegation from the Khazarian Khaganate found us. They were having trouble with a tribe called the Varangians, who'd moved into the lands above them, renamed themselves Rus, and immediately started fighting over the trade routes, which heavily involved the Volga and other rivers. The Khazars were a fascinating people who had ruled that area for over three hundred years by that point. I'd never seen so many unique cultures jammed together."

"Um. I hate to say this, but I've never even *heard* of them. Where were they, in modern terms?"

Dubhghall explained, "You have not heard of them for they are all gone, there's nothing left of that proud culture. The lands they ruled...let's see, today are part of Western Russia, southern Ukraine—but I think Crimea was still in Byzantine hands—and, eh, Kazakhstan I think it's now called. As far as I know, it's like the Khazars never existed; all trace of them is gone.

"But who they were doesn't really matter. At least, it didn't to us at the time. They were just another employer who had a problem for us to solve with our swords and our wits. The people we cared about were these Rus, for you must know about your enemy to kill them most optimally.

"It seems the Varangians were some sort of Nordic people gone a-Viking, who found an area they liked and culturally assimilated so fast that soon they were as Slavic as the people who'd been living there in the first place. They retained that desire to visit their neighbors with predatory intent, however, and so these renamed, reinvented Rus were making enemies in every direction: not just the Khazars, but the Magyars, the Byzantines, the Arabs of the Abbasid Caliphate. *Everyone* from the Euxine Sea (now called the Black Sea) to the *Bahr Khazar* (now we call it the Caspian Sea) hated and feared the Rus. They made trade agreements when they could, but the Rus did not honor them for long, and soon enough there were clashes, and the violence grew into war.

"The Rus were the end of the Khazars. But that was yet to come. At that point, all Zigor and we knew was that a Khazarian Khagan named Joseph was being troubled by a "son of Rurik" named Svyatoslav—as if any of that was supposed to mean something to us.

"By this point in time, we were very full of ourselves. Twenty years of wandering the world, killing all who asked for it (and some who begged for mercy) with little effort had made us swaggering egotists. We could practically live openly as am'r at this time. All the rumor that flew ahead of us as we traveled meant that we could demand to only meet with heads of state at times which suited us—the hours of the night, of course—and our vhoon-drinking only added to the myths of our ferociousness. If we had *not* been barbaric blood-swilling killers, we would only have let people down.

"And we were starting to believe our own hype. Always a dangerous temptation."

"Ha! You say 'starting,' *bróðir minn*, but Zigor had always had, how would you say, over-inflated self-perception." Wulfhram looked condemning; clearly, he did not remember Zigor fondly.

"True! But after being am'r for a while, we ourselves had lost all sense of proportion. We'd met no one who could best us. We just followed Zigor around, taking what we wanted, unstoppable by any kee. Our egos were as bad as his, *mo bhràthair*."

"I...do not like to remember that."

Dubhghall nodded a grave smile. "I know. You know I feel the same. But it's not a long memory, is it? There have been centuries of memories since then."

Wulfhram sat back in his chair again. He visibly wanted no more part in telling the story.

Dubhghall's smile turned wry. He would keep going, but I wondered if even just talking about this point in his life was some kind of penance.

"So...there we were. In Samandar, a city that no longer exists, in a country that no longer exists, making a deal with a ruler who would soon see his empire collapse. We were excited to take on this Svyatoslav. Or Rurik. It wasn't clear if Rurik was still alive or not. Everyone spoke of Svyatoslav as the ruler of the Rus, but it was clear everyone was still afraid of Rurik, who was Svyatoslav's grandfather, or something.

"This really should have tipped us off that we were dealing with another am'r." Wulfhram snorted. Dubhghall continued, his smile even more wryly twisted. "And we had encountered a few am'r, along the way. But Zigor was an aojysht, and we'd met only young am'r, barely stronger than kee. Zigor's strong vhoon-anghyaa made it easy for us to give them each their tokhmarenc—and to walk away with our egos even *more* inflated.

"But all we knew, from our meeting with Joseph and his advisors, was that the leader of the Rus was technically Svyatoslav. And this Rurik was somehow involved—and more feared. But we shrugged it off. So, we had two leaders to fight instead of one. This did not seem like a very big deal. Indeed, if their men were pulled in two directions, loyalties divided, it might end up disappointingly easy to rout the lot of 'em.

"Joseph's commanders told us what they could about the Rus. Essentially, they were still using the Víkingr playbook. The Rus preferred to attack from the water. Indeed, rights to the waterways of the Volga and the Slavutich—now the Dnipro—were what most of the current fuss was about. Rurik, as leader of the Varangians, had supposedly been invited to rule the Slavic tribes of the area. We scoffed at the idea of this—it could only be some sort of rewriting of history for propaganda. But, whatever the true story, Rurik and his followers took hold in Novgorod, a straight shot up the Volga, and next thing their neighbors knew, they'd rebranded as Rus, and were starting out with trading alliances, soon followed up with raids, then followed up by expanding their territory. Whatever they called themselves, they were still going a-Viking. And Joseph was sick of it.

"But Joseph was not the strongest leader. Not the most warrior-like ruler we'd ever met. He was more of a scholar. He seemed more interested in discussing which Jewish kings we'd fought for, and about the Judaism of countries we'd travelled than in giving us useful intelligence about the enemies he was paying us to dispatch for him. It was not a satisfying meeting. But we felt confident, and we were given respect; we were offered a feast, and women for our beds. We passed on the feast and feasted instead on the women.

"Zigor had this...*thing*. He was always trying to get those we fought to do single combat with him. We assumed it was something left over from how ancient he was. Or maybe he was just so wrapped up in his own ego that he preferred everything to be about him."

"And now we shall never know." Wulfhram sounded entirely fine with that.

Dubhghall nodded, and went on, "Most of the time, the other leaders would laugh in his face. And we'd end up fighting three against a warband of thirty—which was unfair odds to them, they'd find out soon enough. Or we'd end up leading a flank of a battle—and stealing all the glory. Things like that.

"But this time, Zigor sent out his stupid invitation...and the response came back with a quickness. Rurik himself would be delighted to meet Zigor on the field of battle, at the time of Zigor's choosing. A location was suggested, which Wulfhram and I went out to scout; it was a wide, flat area of grassland, a good distance from the city. There was no aspect of the landscape one group or the other could use to their advantage. It implied that Rurik was truly invested in this stupid single combat and doing it fairly.

"Now, Zigor was full of himself, but he wasn't stupid. Stupid am'r don't make it to aojysht status. So, despite obvious excitement that he would get his single combat wish fulfilled, he still had Wulfhram and me armor-up, and ride—behind and to either side of him as his liegemen, *blech*—and even, for the look of things, had a company of Khazarian cavalry following behind. Just to show we had official sanction, and for there to be witness to Rurik's demise. Honestly, we all were really there more to witness Zigor's prowess than to be backup."

Wulfhram heaved himself up out his ruminations. "I remember Samandar. It was a pretty city, right on the shores of the Caspian. The Khazarian capital was, what? Atil? But Samandar was perhaps the more charming city. Most of the buildings were built of wood, built with great skill. I remember remarking on the cleverness of their woodwrights and artisans. There were so many houses of worship: Christian and Muslim and Jewish and the followers of Tengri, priests and imams and rabbis and shamans all nattering in the streets. I remember marveling at how many different peoples lived side-by-side in harmony. And all around the city, gardens and vineyards growing every fruit and flower. And busy markets selling spices I'd never smelt before. I remember it was such a lovely place."

Dubhghall looked fondly at his more poetic brother. "Well, what *I* remember is riding out, to meet just after sunset, to what I thought was going to be a most tedious evening. I was concerned that Wulfhram and I would never get to draw our swords, that we must sit in the hot sun in our mail and watch Zigor play with this Rurik for a while, and then dispatch him, with us having had no fun at all. Maybe the Rus would withdraw back whence they came, or maybe they would try to avenge their leader's death, in which case we might have some fun, after all. Mostly, I was afraid of boredom.

"I should have been afraid of everything I knew changing. I should have been afraid of a terrible mortal death, and a terrifying rise from the vistarascha, the awakening to my full am'r life. I should have been afraid of an aojysht who made Zigor seem like a little child playing at soldiers.

"We left the city, traveled through the gardens which my poet over there remembers, and the fields of grain, out into the grassland, and arrived at the agreed-upon location. The Rus were waiting for us.

"Two men sat their horses easily in front of a line of warriors dressed in styles very similar to the ones I'd fought on that stony beach, back on that fateful day. Some Slavic bling had been added, but mostly the Rus still dressed much as their Scandinavian forebears.

"As we got closer, I looked at the two men. One had long dark, thick hair, pulled back in tight braids that ended in knots. The other had a shaved head, with two locks of hair that hung down on either side of his face. The first had olive skin and deep-set dark eyes on either side of an impressive hook of a nose. He had a neatly trimmed beard, but that was no strange thing for the Nordic people, who always took great care with tidiness and cleanliness."

"Why, thank you for noticing, *bróðir minn!*"

"Whit did ah say? Yer'r a muckle gowk, na doubt!" Dubhghall's grin died away, and he slid back into the accentless English. "The other was paler skinned and lighter haired, blue-eyed. He looked like his clothing, where I would have said the first man was from the lands more East and South.

They both used the Slavic that was spoken in those parts, and they also spoke Norsk well enough. The Khazars were so polygot that we'd had no trouble finding a common tongue, although I'd been picking up their version of Turkic. Now, with the Rus, it was just as easy for me and for Zigor, who seemed to be conversant in any language ever spoken.

"Zigor rode forward to the two men. He was sitting proudly on a gorgeous black stallion, full of himself and enjoying the anticipation. Wulfhram and I followed closely, in case things were going to be less boring than I'd feared.

"'I am Zigor,' he announced. 'I am here to test my honor with Lord Rurik.' He looked from one man to the other.

"The darker man replied, 'I am Rurik. This is my grandson, Svyatoslav, leader of the Rus.' I exchanged glances with Wulfhram. He did not look any older than his supposed grandson. And his grandson was passive, while Rurik was clearly the one in charge. Neither of us liked it.

"Zigor was sniffing the air curiously. 'I eshteshcinyast...tell me, how do I know you? What is your vhoon-anghyaa?'

"Rurik laughed. 'You should know me, youngling. I am the Aojysht-of-aojyshtaish!'

"We all glanced around at each other, confused. Finally, Zigor inquired, 'Is that not the one named Egnatius? I have met him. Or has he met his tokhmarenc, the final ending of that long existence?'

"Rurik went from self-important to livid in an instant. 'The one who currently goes by Egnatius is old, yes. But he claims that title without having ascertained he *is* the oldest. One day I will show him who is the true Aojysht-of-aojysh-taish!'

"There was a pause. We were all pretty sure Egnatius was truly the Aojysht-of-aojyshtaish. For one, every am'r had heard of him, and from their entry into the am'r life, had heard tales of him. It seemed unlikely that every single am'r we'd ever met was getting it *wrong*.

"We had all been scenting the air, by this point. Rurik was definitely an aojysht. I was still only am'r-nafsh, and still pretty ignorant, but even I could tell *that*. Rurik's vhoon-anghyaa had a strangely familiar tang, once I was focused on it, but, well, honestly, I didn't have enough information to work with. I turned to Zigor, who *did* have that knowledge. But he'd shrugged the whole thing off. He just wanted to get to fighting, and if this strange am'r wanted to claim to be the eldest of us all, well, what did that matter? The day's fight had just been taken up a notch. Fighting another am'r was more of a challenge than fighting a kee, even if the am'r was more than a little delusional."

Listening, I felt my body go rigid. If I could still have broken out in a cold sweat, I would have. "Wait! That can't be! But it sounds like..."

Dubhghall laughed mirthlessly. "Oh, it *was*. Your old friend Kurgan. The Egnatius he spoke of was what Bagamil called himself, back then. And Good Ol' Kurgan was going by Rurik. And, while he was living in secrecy in the step-pelands, he definitely had his grudge against Bagamil in full measure."

"But...if he was still hiding himself from Bagamil...why did he so easily tell you who he was?" My head was swimming. It didn't matter if this was thousands of years in the past. Any mention of Kurgan made me feel queasy and uncomfortable.

"Well, he didn't get into all the details. He could have simply been boasting, something which am'r have been known to do. He didn't give us his whole history, or anything. So, even if we'd just walked away from the encounter, all we'd remember was we'd met some batshit crazy am'r in Rus-lands who claimed it was really he who was the Aojysht-of-aojyshtaish. Something to be forgotten before we'd ridden to the next adventure.

"But he wasn't planning on letting us ride away. He intended to bring us all to our final ends, so telling us *anything* wasn't a problem, to his mind. That information was only going to the grave."

That sounded like the Kurgan I'd known. Except. "Uh, Kurgan was not someone I'd've thought was into a fair fight. In fact, I remember him *specifically* telling me that am'r never fight fair." *Am'r-splaining, really. What an asshole.*

"Now *you* are getting ahead of my story, lassie. But, no, Kurgan/Rurik was not planning any sort of fairness.

"Zigor still wanted his one-on-one; his ego was that big. But, as I've said, he wasn't entirely stupid, so he did take us aside beforehand and say to keep an eye on Rurik and Rurik's men. Which we were happy to do. To be painfully honest, *I* was the stupid one, back then. I was happy that it seemed like it wouldn't be a boring day, after all. I felt pleased with the anticipation that things would be more complicated than Zigor dispatching Rurik with ease, and us riding off with our reward."

"We were both young and dumb. Too full of ourselves. I do not like to remember any of this, I already said."

"I find myself reticent to tell this part of the story, as well, *mo bhràthair*. I had thought all emotion had long since drained away. But no—it *hurts* to remember this, *richt enuff*. But I will finish the tale for Noosh. Perhaps it will lead to a new healing.

"*Weel. Sae…*Wulfhram and I fell back, with the almost-forgotten Zhazarian calvary unit. And the equally-forgotten Svyatoslav fell back with his band, to watch from their side.

"Zigor and Rurik had dismounted. There was no benefit to a duel on horseback. I'd passed the reins back to one of the Khazars, to keep my own hands free. We stayed mounted in case we needed to get to Zigor in a hurry.

"The combatants walked to meet each other. Zigor saluted, wanting every drop of formality from the experience. Rurik returned a lazy half-assed salute, more an expression of "Yeah, yeah, yeah, whatever," than a gesture of respect.

"There was a pause. And then they both attacked at the same instant. I won't bore you with what I remember of the blow-by-blow. Suffice it to say, Rurik played with Zigor like a cat with a mouse, until he grew bored. Then, moving faster than even the am'r eye could follow, he took off Zigor's head with a too-easy sweep of his sword.

"Zigor's head barely had time to bounce once on the ground, when, without a command needed from Rurik, the entire group of Rus turned on us.

"Svyatoslav led the kee Rus fighters to take down our Khazarian cavalry. Ah—Svyatoslav was am'r, and clearly of Rurik's direct vhoon-anghyaa. He had been a perfect subordinate the whole time, and their batch of kee obeyed him like robots. There was clearly a lot of am'r influence happening there. Svyatoslav and his men had, after Zigor had been beheaded, swung round and were easily mopping up our Khazarian escort, who'd not had enough time to try to escape. I assume they died, to a man.

"Their archers, who had been the main downfall of the Khazarian company, also shot our horses from under us. I don't know if they were aiming at us and just hit the horses because they were a bigger target, or if they were just trying to unhorse us, but the end result was both *mo bhràthair* and I getting out from under dying horses as fast as we could, to escape injury or just being trapped and easily dispatched.

"But I didn't have time to consider any of that, then. Wulfhram and I were shortly discovering what it was like to be on the losing side of a two-on-one combat—when the one was kicking the arses of the two.

"I'd never seen anything like it. *Mo faol-chù* and I were reasonably skilled fighters before we became am'r-nafsh. And since then, we had been trained by Zigor and practicing more than regularly. We should have, the two of us, been able to hold our own against one full am'r.

"But Rurik was everywhere, every second. He would be fully engaged with Wulfhram bearing down hard upon him with his beloved sword—broad-bladed and able to cut through bone, and even other swords, on occasion!—and

I would quietly slide into where his blind-spot should be, to surprise him. But he refused to be surprised! With a too-lithe spin, he would damn near knock my own sword from my hand, and then spin back around to meet Wulfhram's next thrust.

It didn't matter how we changed-up our styles. He met us each with apparent prescience. He was strong like we'd never known possible. We were both meeting him with two swords; he was likewise armed—"

Wulfhram popped into the conversation again. "I had my Mjǫtuðr and a lovely seax named Hjartabroti: Heartbreaker. I loved them both, and they had been almost extensions of myself for many a battle."

"What were *your* swords named?" I asked Dubhghall.

"Ah, I had less poetry in my blood then. Zigor had given me a longer sword since I'd joined him. He'd made me practice with her until I learned my new am'r-naf-sh strength. I'd named her Siùrsach, because she'd been a bitch to learn…but also turned out to be a *useful* bitch against my enemies. I still had Pointeach, my sweet short sword as well.

"But back to what I was saying—and this is the insane part. We were coming at him with our four swords, doing wide sweeps with both our swords. And he was just knocking all swords down with these slashes of unimaginable power. I was not a weakling and Wulfhram was taller and far more muscled than he. But it didn't matter. Every time our swords met his, he practically knocked them out of our hands. And that was dangerous, because he was also fast—too fast. If I opened myself up for even an instant, he was pressing his advantage.

"How could we two strong, well-trained, combat-tested fighters be losing so unquestionably to this one man? The answer is easy to figure out now, but in the heat of battle, and after our years of experience being the most power-ful and unstoppable, it was creating this confusion in my brain. A warrior needs to be clear-minded during battle, able to process information and act on it without conscious thought. But this confusion was slowing me down, and filling me with a fear I'd not known since that that fateful fight on the beach.

"With that confusion and fear driving me, I wanted this fight over. I decided it was time to end things, before it got any worse. In a moment when I thought Rurik was truly solely focused on Wulfhram, I—moving as fast as I ever had in my life—lunged in a paired strike, Siùrsach aimed for his throat, and Pointeach craving to set the organs in his belly free.

"But, moving even faster than I, Rurik impossibly side-stepped my lunge. And as momentum brought me into his space, he shoved me directly into Wulfhram.

"Wulfhram had been about to follow my attack, his Mjǫtuðr raised high, and when I crashed into him, it left him in an all-too vulnerable position. Rurik took this seconds-long opportunity to shift smoothly to the side and as part of that movement throw an offside shot against Wulfhram's arm that still held Mjǫtuðr aloft.

"Things were moving almost too fast for me to follow. As his arm holding his beloved sword fell away from his body, Wulfhram shoved me to the side, protecting me from Rurik's sword, which, using the same downward momentum, would have crashed down into my spine in the next instant.

"Wulfhram's never been one to let the little things—like a lost dominant arm!—bother him. While I was still catching up with what had just happened, he dropped to his knee and sliced deep into Rurik's left thigh with Hjartabroti, then rolled forward into a tumble, seemingly as graceful as if he wasn't spurting blood from his right arm.

"As he rolled, blood spun out and caught in the twilight like a little whirlwind of garnets. We could all smell that fresh blood very acutely; it spurred both Rurik and me to a greater intensity."

Dubhghall nodded to me. "I know you know the concept of 'death from below'—as fighters on the smaller side, it's a useful trick for both of us. And I tried it then, as Rurik seemed slightly distracted by the scent of blood filling the air. I bent low and Pointeach again sought out the soft places under his mail, while Siùrsach flew up offhand, seeking to meet his blades and keep them occupied.

"But that too fast, too powerful motherfucker blocked first my upper sword thrust, then the impetus crashed the lower blade away as well. Siùrsach was knocked from my hand with that power-block, and Pointeach was knocked straight down. I was left bent over, my mail-clad back yet again all-too-exposed.

"This time, there was no one to block the downward stroke that severed my spinal column. I dropped like a stone. My head shifted as I fell, so at least I did not just fall right onto my face.

"From that terribly incapacitated position, I could just manage to follow what happened next. Wulfhram was running at Rurik, screaming, and crashed into him with the shoulder missing the arm. He tried with his seax to slam that momentum into Rurik's guts.

"Rurik's mail parted under the thrust of Hjartabroti, and the blade finally found a home in his bowels...but at the cost of Rurik's longer sword driving deep into Wulfhram's own core.

"Rurik shoved him backwards, flipped his own shorter sword up and catching it—reversed in his grasp for greater force—drove it into my brother's heart."

Dubhghall stopped. Took a few deep breaths. They both had that grey cast to their skin that am'r get when they are doing badly: usually physically, but I'd seen it caused by extreme emotion before. In this moment, I felt really shitty for asking them to tell me the whole story. It wasn't like I didn't *know* that all am'r origin stories have a mortal death at their center.

"*Weel. Sae.* At that point I had some time to catch up with my own pain—which was there, but it was a very strange kind of pain, like nothing I'd felt before. More *real* was seeing my brother crumpled, contorted on the ground. Rurik had tugged his swords from Wulfhram's body and walked idly away, satisfied by the day's events.

"I never lost consciousness. Some nerve endings kept running to my brain. So I was able to watch Rurik's men build a fire with as much kindling as they could find. It was not much—we were in grassland, remember, and the building of Samandar had felled whatever forests had once been there. However, as you know, am'r bodies burn much more readily than kee, and Zigor's ancient flesh was the best kindling around. They started with him at the center, and once the blaze was roaring, I got the *joy* of first watching my brother get dragged into the conflagration, and then feel it happening to myself.

"The burning was so painful that I will not try to describe it to you. But just because it did not leave scars across my am'r skin does not mean those scars are not there in my mind."

I'd been taking all this in with an all-too-intense empathy, but there was a question too irresistible to hold in. "Doesn't fire kill us *dead?* Tokhmarenc-level-dead? Like, even if you're am'r-nafsh, you-don't-get-to-rise-in-the-vis-tarascha-dead?"

"What, lass, d'you wish we'd never made it back to bore you with our tedious tale?" Dubhghall saw my face and immediately stopped teasing. "Naw, naw, dinnae tak' it lik' that!" He continued, "I must admit, I was surprised, myself, when I woke up. Although the hunger was upon me, and I didn't stop to ask questions for a good long while. Ach, what hunger that was! I likely devastated a village, all mindless and bestial.

"But *then* I stopped to think and to question. How did I survive the blaze that should have ended me before I truly began? And I do not to this day know the answer, not fully. But my best guess is this: Rurik had left before Wulfhram and I were even fully dragged onto the pyre. He gloated over Zigor—another aojysht—*bit he didn't gie a bugger aboot twa no-name am'r-nafsh lik' us.*

"With Rurik and his influence gone, the underlings did a half-assed job. They likely didn't bother to drag us to the hottest area (that would be where Zigor was burning up like his own private supernova). Perhaps they knocked aside the wood and grass cuttings by simply dragging us to just inside the circumference of the flame.

"And the underlings did not stay to toast the Tenth Century equivalent of s'mores over us, I'd bet. They just wodged us in there and went back to whatever they had been doing before Rurik did his little demonstration—more of a wank than a fight, as much as it hurts me to admit it.

"And my guess is that am'r-nafsh, not being fully am'r, don't incinerate with the same *enthusiasm* as proper am'r do. If that's the case, they *should* have stayed around and added more fuel when our fire extinguished, with the two of us only partly burned. But Rurik's underlings were long gone.

"And *then*, what I think happened after that, is that a band of nomads came across our charred bodies and came to the reasonable assumption we were quite dead. We had died the mortal death, that's for sure. The Khazars had some cities, but most still lived as nomads, so it's not a stretch that a roving company would trip over us.

"They were compassionate people. They buried us. Or at least, Wulfhram and me. There would not have been anything of Zigor left, just some particularly fine ash. But through the kindness of strangers, we made it down into the safety of the earth, the protection of darkness and gentle soil, and there we could begin the transformation of the vistarascha.

"I rose first—"

"*Já*, you were always an overeager bastard—"

Dubhghall rolled his eyes. "It says nothing about me that I woke first. But this eejit has never gotten over it. And he should feel no jealousy—"

"I'm not jealous—!"

"AND he should feel no jealousy, because let me tell you, that was the worst period of my life. First, the terrible hungers of the vistarascha. But at least that time was a mindless blur. Once I came to myself, I have never felt so terribly alone. My brother was gone. My mentor—and for all his faults, he had taught us well—was gone. I'd gone through the greatest transformation one can survive, and I was utterly alone.

"I found clothing in the houses of my victims to replace my charred rags. I found a replacement knife and acceptable sword. I liberated two horses, and I made my way back to where I had emerged from my impromptu grave. The signs of our burning were gone from the grasslands, but the location was burned—and I say this *literally*—into my memory.

"I started digging. I could see the disturbed dirt from where I arisen from my vistarascha, and I dug first to one side of me and then the other, every few feet. I cannot tell you how many holes I dug, desperately hoping to find *mo faol-chù*. I found only the bones of our Khazarian escort. I dug all night, and when the sun rose, I made one of the holes bigger, and covered myself with dirt, and went back into the ground for the day.

"As the sun set, I dug myself out and started again. On that second day, I finally found him. They'd buried him nice and deep, for which I thank those unknown good people. I reburied him, marked the spot in a subtle way, so as not to arouse any suspicions if other nomads wandered past, and I rode to the nearest people I could find, for sustenance and preparation—the nearest village, you will remember, was now a ghost village, because, as the local legend already had it, an evil ghoul had ravaged it. Remembering that time, I will not say they were wrong.

"I came across another band of nomads. Nomads are generally people who hold the ancient custom of hospitality to the stranger, so I was brought in, given a chance to bathe, and fed, all without any questions as to who I was or where I was from. I can't have looked—or smelled—the sort of person you'd want to welcome to your tent, but then, these nomads were armed with sword and knife, and they became very dangerous people if they felt even slightly threatened. So we got along perfectly; I honored them for their hospitality, and they fed me and caught me up with recent events.

"Of which there had been many. It seemed that Joseph was Khagan no longer. The Rus under Svyatoslav had made good on their threats and a terrible battle had been fought. Joseph had fled his Empire. It was rumored that he'd fled west, trying to make it to the Byzantine empire, and that Svyatoslav was hunting him down. The people I was with had at best a mild interest in such things, however. They just wanted to be left alone to get on with the rhythm of their lives, which had gone on unchanged and unchanging in uncountable generations back through the three hundred years of the Khazars, and the people who came before them, and the people who came before them. They called themselves Khazars now, but they would shrug that off and call themselves whatever they needed to, if they would just be left alone to guide their herds across the land in the old patterns.

"I left those good people in the evening and returned to Wulfhram's grave. He did not arise, but I had acquired the materials to erect a small yurt, which I could rest in during the day, and in which I stored items for when my brother returned to me.

"I had also acquired a woman to be my izchha, the blood-donor I lay with, as I waited. If I ever knew her name, I forgot it as soon as possible. All I cared about was seeing that one patch of earth stir with a beloved body restless under it.

"It was not many nights before I got my wish. I was sitting out under the stars, and the woman was chattering to me in her own language, which I knew well enough but was not interested in what she was saying. And then my total attention was caught by a shifting of the earth under the light of stars and moon. I cried out with delight and ran to help scoop the dirt off my brother.

"He came out as I expected: ravenous. The woman had screamed and fled into the yurt when it was clear a dead person was rising from the grave. Natural curiosity had brought her back out, and Wulfhram's crazed eyes fixed on her before he even recognized me. She was dead and drained not long after.

"It sounds terrible to you, I expect. But we were not very near any other kee, and my reasoning was, if there was only one, perhaps one would suffice to satiate him enough to find sanity again, and he need not massacre a whole village, as I had done."

"And for this I am eternally grateful," Wulfhram added. "For I was capable of endless savagery when I rose from the vistarascha, and my brother had the foresight to prevent it, and prevent centuries of regret thereafter. I may be a fighter, one who has gone a-Víking, but I am a thinking, feeling man, not a beast."

"Aye, ye ainlie need fear us wee ones." Dubhghall's dubious sense of humor could not be stifled long. "Anyways, that's our tale. Well, the tale of us becoming am'r. But I won't go into the next thousand plus years. Not without a *drink*, at least. Talking is thirsty work..."

"*Já, Já*, that it is. I thirst, as well."

I was ready to listen to every story they had...but I didn't feel quite ready to go out for *drinks* with the lads. I still was not-entirely-comfortable with the memory of Lilani with the sweet kee Nadia in that pub loo—and that had been entirely non-kill-y.

We all stood and stretched, even though am'r bodies don't get stiff and achy like kee ones; some habits die hard.

I had a few last questions, of course. "Once you knew about Kurgan, why did you never tell Bagamil?"

"We didn't know he was Kurgan. We only knew him as Rurik. Some insane aojysht. And we never saw him again. So we didn't know if he had been given a very deserving tokhmarenc already."

"But...why didn't you go after him for vengeance?"

"Well, we did talk about it. Many a night, at first. But we did not hold any real love for Zigor, so we felt no need to avenge him. And at this time, it was pretty common for the aojysht of an area to kill any strange am'r who impinged upon their territory, as discouragement to others. Rurik was claiming the lands of the Khazars, and that's how most of the am'r would do it, as well. It was only some am'r who never settled down and spent their lives travelling, such as Bagamil, who didn't engage in such behavior. So we didn't hold a grudge, and we couldn't blame him. *Better tae juist jook th' mental numpty, ye ken?*"

I couldn't help but wish they'd told Sandu or Bagamil about the "numpty" in the intervening centuries. It would have made *my* life a lot easier.

"What matters, *Frøken* Noosha, is that we survived his best efforts to destroy us. And that we have had all the time since to be brothers."

"Aye, not brothers of the same mother, but brothers in blood, a stronger, surer bond. I would not do anything differently, if it risked changing my life so that I haven't gotten to have this big blonde bawbag driving me crazy."

"So, what happened after you were reunited?"

"After? We just fought our way home. We knew each other's styles, we'd gotten used to each other's company. We loved each other, although at first we did not really understand how much. When we got back to the coast of Lower Lotharingia, we had one final night of reveling, and then I went back to my home, and he to his."

"*Já*. We had both a strong longing for our families, and for a way of life we both had come to miss, constantly travelling through strange lands and full of stranger peoples."

"Aye, we had perhaps idealized our kee lives. And Zigor had never specifically mentioned to us that there was no going back to the kee world—it would have never occurred to him to be around kee for any reason other than to fuck them, drink from them, or kill them in battle."

"And there was that dogged refusal of his to never go anywhere near the lands of his birth."

"Aye, we never did find out the reason for that. And never will now! Anyways, to make a long and sad story short, once we got 'home,' we discovered we could not fit back in to the kee world. Most everyone who remembered us was already dead—and those who weren't refused to believe that our unageing selves were the same men who died on that stony beach. And my world had changed even more distressingly: it was no longer being called Pictland and the Scoti tribes were rapidly taking over the culture, language, everything. Indeed, my clan had already begun leaving the lands I knew, moving west to where they still are today. Everything was more foreign than the furthest lands we'd visited.

"So I got away from there, *as fleet as maybee aye*, and I wandered the world, a lone mercenary. It was a dark time. I could not go back to the lands I knew like my own body, be laird of my clan—in my youthful am'r pride I assumed that I would be—and watch the generations come up around me. So I was undoubtedly a sullen bastard to everyone I met. Which did not get in the way of being a mercenary—indeed, it was effective advertising.

"Some years later, I was on a battlefield, some minor skirmish between a Byzantine duchy and a Lombard principality. There was a lot of work for a mercenary on the Italian peninsula in the 1000s. Anyways, I get the feeling another am'r is there, on the other side. '*Och guid!*' I think, 'Finally some real fun!' I cut my way through the kee soldiers in between us. And when I get there? Who do I eshteshcinyast...*bit th' muckle Northman ah used tae ken sae weel.*"

"I was in the same boat, as they say. My family would not recognize me, and I would have had to kill them if I had not left in a hurry. Hurting and lonely, I wandered the world, and I had only one skill that anyone wanted to hire, only one thing that made the pain go away. Until I again saw this *litilmenni* across a battlefield."

"What did you do?"

"What do you think, lassie? We immediately dropped our financial allegiances and killed everyone who took offense to that. And then we hugged, we found some still living wounded and drained them dry for the vhoon-vayon, the healing by blood, and we've never been apart since.

"Well, *mostly*. Sometimes he or I get a longing for the landscapes of our kee lives. And technically, I am the most senior am'r for what is now called Scotland, and he for Norway, so sometimes business calls us to attend to matters separately. But if we can be, we are together and we deal with problems together.

"It's a lonely thing, being am'r. Why would one choose to spend all those years just cycling through frithaputhraish. They are fine and all—we've had some fun over the years—but I have someone who can truly understand me." Dubhghall met my eyes, "I know you love them. But can you truly say you *understand* Sandu? Bagamil?"

I didn't like that question. I put off answering as long as I could. "I wish I could say yes, but no, of course I can't. That's why you asked me. I'm from such a different time, such a different kee world from them. Sometimes they feel so alien to me."

"Aye, that's my point. I have someone who truly *gets* me. He kens me, and I truly comprehend all of him. Just because we are not the finest *nutrition* for each other should not, does not, decrease our bond."

"Almost none of the other am'r are able to work like that," I noted.

"And maybe that's what's wrong with us as a species," Dubhghall grinned. "Maybe the am'r-am'r-nafsh bond holds us back, keeps us solitary and untrusting as we have been all these millennia. I do not know, I am not some am'r philosopher. If anyone can begin to know, it will be *you*, archivist-to-the-am'r, holder of our stories and our secrets."

"All I know," Wulfhram concluded, "is that *we* have done things the right way for *us*. And that is all that matters, I think."

NOTE ON BLOOD BROTHERS

Again, from the minute Noosh and I met Wulfhram and Dubhghall (pronounced "Doo-gul," if you were wondering!) in the Rave Cave, I've always wanted to find out their backstories. How these two enemies became lifelong friends (and an am'r lifelong friend is a whole 'nother level of friendship!) was always a story I wanted to hear—and then tell! This really was a treat, and not just because I wrote a big chunk of it during a week of a solo writing retreat in New Orleans, fueling myself with amazing Creole and Cajun food and sitting by a pretty pool.

Thanks as always to Trent Stewart for helping me choreograph the fight scenes—one of the most fun parts of writing! Huge thanks to my Old Norse editor Olaf Haraldson, to my Pictish editor Justin Davis, and to my Modern Scottish editor Jen Darling. They all helped me make sure the historical and linguistic details were accurate, but if there are any mistakes remaining, that's all on me, of course.

Not many more things need to said about this story, except that it's basically a violent romp through the 900s, and this is exactly why I love writing this series so much. Obviously, this story takes place in the world of the Blood & Ancient Scrolls Series, and the frame of this story takes place sometime after Book III, Blood Ad Infinitum, but it's not specific to any other points in Noosh's timeline, except that she's obviously in her Library at the underground Castle Dracula, not bouncing around the world on am'r-ish adventure.

ABYSSINIA

It was one of those impossibly, intolerably muggy Philly summer nights.

There's no breeze on nights like these, but just in case the air might move the tiniest bit, she was sitting out on the battered square of a back porch, drinking a pilfered bottle of Babbo's grappa.

She could steal his grappa because Babbo didn't really like the stuff. He had to pretend to because it was Italian, and Babbo was as proud of being Napoletano as a person could be. At every gifting occasion, neighbors and the men from the union would proudly offer him bottles of grappa smuggled in from the Old World, and he would welcome them with cries of joyful thanks. And then later they would collect dust in the back of the liquor cabinet, while the bathtub gin and moonshine never needed wiping off.

Prohibition might be the law of the land, but dry laws never seemed to have impacted anyone she knew. No one in the neighborhood was narking to the flatfoots because *everyone* boozed, male and female alike. Indeed, there was a chapter of Women's Organization for National Prohibition *Reform* that met at the Baptist church down the corner.

The first time she'd stolen a bottle, she'd thought grappa tasted like gasoline. But at least it was *free* gasoline. And now she even liked the harsh bite—it made you know you were drinking something. And it was even better with a cigarette, when she could afford to splurge on a pack of Luckys or was offered a loosey. It had to be offered though. She was too proud to ask.

And tonight she *needed* the giggle juice and a snipe. It had been a hard, damn day. And then a hard, damn night. Her hand shook a little when she picked up the bottle to take another swig.

She'd taken another gal to see Emma after work. It wasn't an easy one. After she'd helped that poor thing home, she'd barely been able to get herself home. She didn't like to cry where people could see. You looked like a *pathetic frail,* like you had no pride. She didn't have *much,* but she did have plenty of pride. Babbo had taught her that. If you were born with the name Vitale, you had the Vitale pride. One of her teachers, before she'd left school to get the National Biscuit Company factory job to help out because Mamma was having another baby, had told her that her name had come down from the ancient Romans, and it meant *life.* *"Certo!"*

Babbo had boomed when she'd told him, but she could tell he hadn't thought of it before, and it made him even more proud.

"And you *are* vital, so full of life," came the softest whisper from the darkness of the alley, and she almost knocked the bottle of grappa down the steps. She had to take a second to decide if she was hearing things.

"I got a knife!" she called out and reached for the switchblade in the pocket she'd sewn into her dress.

"You do not need a knife with me, sister," came the voice, still low as if gentling a scared animal, but also low for a woman, a warm contralto.

It made her want to relax into it right away, but that feeling scared her even more, so she thumbed the little round switch. The blade sprang out.

"No, no," the voice assured her, as the female shape, which until this moment had merely been a darker shadow, slid close enough to make out details. The shadow woman was what men would call a "butter and egg fly," filling out a thin-pleated black dress with perfect round curves. Her skin was a rich honey bronze, and her glam pin curls were the same honey shade.

"I am impressed with your defenses," the dusky dame promised in her low tones, "but I am no threat to you, Palmina."

"How do you know my name?"

"Everyone in the neighborhood knows you. I simply had to ask."

"Well, why d'ya ask then?"

"Why would I not want to get to know such an impressive woman as yourself?"

"Ahhh, stop! Why're you saying these things to me? Nobody from here talks like you. What d'ya want? *Really*."

"You are astute as well as brave. There is indeed something I want from you—"

"I knew it!"

"But now that I have met you, I want your friendship, as well."

"That ain't how friendship works, lady."

"I know how friendship works, sweet girl. Give me a chance to earn your friendship, please."

Palmina looked at the stranger. From the shadows, she was *shady* in every sense. But she was compelling too. The pleated dress and matching boxy jacket were probably silk, the way they glistened in the low light from the windows above the sides of the alley. The woman didn't wear a hat or gloves, but her shoes were brand-new, black leather Cuban-heeled oxfords with a delicate pattern of perforations. She was well-to-do, but she wasn't stuck-up fancy. A woman could tell so many things about another woman from her clothes and shoes. Makeup and hair also told stories. While the woman had perfectly waved hair, she wore almost no face paint. Her skin was so flawless that Palmina had to assume she wore foundation, but her eyebrows were not plucked Hollywood thin, nor drawn in, and she wore no eyeshadow. She *must* have put mascara on, but just that and perfect carmine lips. She still looked like a movie star, regardless, not like anyone she'd ever met before.

Palmina found herself wanting to hear this woman's story, so she pushed aside what was otherwise perfectly reasonable mistrust. "I never had a friend whose name I didn't even know."

"Ah, a very good point. My name is Astryiah."

"Ahh-stree-yah?"

"That is it exactly. However, most Americans do not seem able to say it. I have been telling people my name is Alyssa. They seem more capable of pronouncing that."

"Astryiah's beauteeful! Where's it from?"

"Thank you, sweet one. And what a subtle way to find out about me. Your diplomacy shall be rewarded. I come from a country which in your Bible is called Judah. It is now called Palestine, and against all reason or logic, it is ruled by the British. In essence, I have no home."

Palmina had known the woman was foreign, but this was vastly more exotic than anything she would have guessed.

This Astryiah had seemed coolly unemotional, despite her stated, and obvious, desire to make friends with Palmina. But when she'd said "I have no home," Palmina could hear the depths of emotion under the simplicity of the words.

"I'm sorry to hear that," was all she could say, but she could also hold out the grappa bottle as a tangible form of comfort.

"This is very kind of you." Astryiah took the bottle, and somehow in the process, Palmina found herself scrunching over to make space for her on the top step. It would have been too much to call the cramped space a *porch*; it was just five rickety steps up to the back door with a railing on one side that you grabbed at risk of splinters at best and complete structural failure at worst.

As the shadow lady settled so close beside Palmina that their hips were touching, she handed the bottle back. Palmina took a swig and put the cap back on before she realized the woman hadn't bothered to take a sip. Well, that wasn't a surprise. Many people found grappa to have a taste reminiscent of paint thinner, her Babbo included. She put the bottle down between her feet.

"Astryiah," she said, the name still tasting so strange in her mouth, "I kinda wouldn't mind knowing why you're sitting on these steps with me. *Besides* being my 'friend'."

"It is because we are friends that I will tell you, *chamuda*. I am unused to telling my business to anyone...but I do desire to share with you.

"I have been in this country...some while now." Astryiah waved an elegant hand to dismiss the value of mentioning any specific length of time. "Since I am a woman without a home, I thought it good to come to a country that thinks only of the future. This new Philadelphia is a vibrant place where a stranger can fit in to the bustle and thrum of human life."

That was an odd way to phrase things. But then again, this woman was unlike anyone she'd met before. And she was *foreign*. Foreigners could be expected to say things strangely, English not being their first language and all. Why, her Nonna and Nonno could barely even speak English. Astryiah spoke it better than they did, by far. She talked better than some of the kids she'd grown up with, American-born and all.

The pause in the conversation gave Palmina a chance to enjoy the warm glow of the grappa in her mind and body, relaxing for the first time all day. She was also acutely aware of Astryiah's hip and thigh pressing against her own. The sultry night air seemed right for this moment, despite the trickle of sweat down her back, despite the damp stickiness of her bra against her skin.

"As your friend-to-be, may I ask what has been troubling you on this hot summer night, so like the nights in the land of my birth? Summer is the time to be carefree in this country, is it not? Dances, cookouts, and...I do not know... parades?"

Palmina laughed. "Parades mostly happen during day-time. Don't they have those things where you come from?"

"Cookouts were nothing special to my people; we cooked outdoors generally. I have been to parades, but they were always—shall we say—*military* in nature. I haven't danced in...many, many years."

"But that just ain't right! Dancing is...I dunno...you just can't *not!* Hold up!" Palmina ran into the house and started the record player. She'd had enough extra pennies last week to buy a 45 of Artie Shaw's "Begin the Beguine." She left the back door open and, made brave by the booze, as she ran down the wobbly steps she grabbed Astryiah's hand and pulled her out into the alley.

"I...I do not know how to dance to this music—" Astryiah began.

Palmina just laughed, settled the one elegant bronze hand onto her shoulder, and held the other outstretched with her own. Taking the lead, she spun them through the torrid shadows.

Her unexpected visitor brought an equally unexpected new pattern to Palmina's life, which had felt full enough already. Every day she got up painfully early for the bus ride that ended when the conductor yelled, "Pick Me Up Central! All you *working* men and women get out here!" with a leer on his face. It was assumed that because the National Biscuit Company employed women as well as men, that affairs between employees were inevitable. Whether it was a self-fulfilling prophecy or not, it wasn't wrong.

Then it was a full day boxing Lorna Doones, Oreo Cookies, and Fig Newtons—and staying out of the river of drama that flowed through the factory. After all that, she had her... other job. And then when she got home from *that*, most evenings she'd find Astryiah waiting for her.

She took Astryiah to some jolly-ups, for her shadow lady turned out to be a natural jitterbug, a jive bomber. Palmina derived great satisfaction watching the boys who fancied themselves real cool cats trying to impress a dame who so clearly outclassed them. Astryiah treated them all with good-humored dismissal, not hostile, but clearly not welcoming to unwanted attentions. Palmina took notes, because she'd always found men far more of a hassle than Astryiah seemed to. Although after the first attempt to introduce Astryiah by her real name, she quickly fell back on "Alyssa." No one else seemed to be able to handle it, although that could be because it was hard to really hear anything anyone said when the joint was jumpin'.

On other nights, they just stayed in, spun some platters, and talked. Astryiah was a true world traveler, although many places she had visited—"oh, quite some time ago"—with that same airy, elegantly dismissive wave of the hand. But she would still answer Palmina's eager questions. Not all of them, but enough.

"You have never left this country, not even to go to the land of your ancestors? But no, so few people get a chance to travel, most especially not women. You would make an excellent traveler, *chamuda*. I would love the chance to show you around the world."

Astryiah would often say ridiculous things like that. Palmina ignored the obviously impossible as a matter of course.

Astryiah apparently never slept. Palmina had never minded the occasional late night in the past, but as the weeks went on with her conversations with her late-night friend ending regularly sometime around sunrise, Palmina began to feel the lack of sleep taking its toll. To her surprise, she had an attack of the whips and jangles.

"Astryiah—I love our nights. But can we skip 'em for a bit?"

"If you are enjoying them, why stop?"

"Because I'm joed! Uh, that's slang. I mean I'm just too worn out these days to handle everything I gotta handle."

"You have talked *around* all the things you must handle. I know about the factory. I know about how much your family demands from you. But there is a third thing, a very big thing, and it drains you more than just staying up talking with me. Have we not grown close enough that you might share it with me...?"

"You don't wanna hear about this. It's not nice."

"*Chamuda*... I have seen far more terrible things in this world than you can imagine. Tell me. Maybe I can help."

"How could you help with this? You're a stranger. I mean, you're not from the neighborhood. The gals wouldn't know they could trust you. They trust me because they know me."

"I see. And this is a problem where only women can help women?"

Palmina paused. She didn't talk about this part of her life. Not with anyone who wasn't already involved. Would speaking of it to Astryiah be a betrayal? But Astryiah seemed to be understanding it already, so she said, "Yes."

"Oh, my dear one. This is no new problem for women. We have always had to help ourselves with this, for men are never help."

"You dig what I'm sayin'?"

"Of course I understand. Listen. The city I come from; in ancient times, there were whorehouses. Not like they are today, dirty and shameful. No, the women were respected as providing an important service. In times further past, they had been admired as acolytes of the Goddess, and some of that respect still was attached to their trade.

"But when women and men have pleasure together, there will be results. And these women were not desirous of raising all these results. These women did not have time to be mothers, at least not at this stage in their lives. They were what you might call "businesswomen," and they had their careers to attend to.

"There was a bathhouse attached to their establishment. The women and their clients enjoyed the warm bath, hot bath, cold plunge, and steam room. There were masseurs and even barbers. But there was also a woman who sold certain herbs for women who found themselves...in that condition. She would give you the herbs, and then if you grew very sick from them, she would nurse you.

"And it was not just the women of this house who used her services. Women from all classes, all ranks of life—from the richest senators' wives to the lowliest serving girls—all found their way to this woman, because there is a right time for love to turn into new life, but there are also times when it would be very bad indeed."

Palmina sat through this outflowing of words, frozen by their unexpectedness.

Astryiah continued, "So, you see, *chamuda*, I understand this matter well. There has never been a time when a woman could fail to understand it. And seldom indeed have there been times when men have kept their desire for power and control—and their unwanted noses—out of this private, personal business of women."

"Oh." It was all Palmina could say. Why was she so shocked to hear Astryiah's words? Of course every woman around the world had this in common. She'd never thought about women in other countries, but then she really didn't have time to think, because she was always so busy trying to keep *her* gals safe.

No, it was silly to be shocked. And it would be foolish to see if Astryiah didn't have some knowledge that would help her.

"I'm not…the woman with the herbs, like back in your old days. I just help fems who need it. They know to come to me. And I set up a time and place, and the woman who has the know-how to fix it meets us there. I hold my gals' hands while it happens. I hold 'em while they cry. I make sure they aren't too sick to make it home. Sometimes they doss here overnight. Sometimes they cry all night, and I stay up with 'em. I cry with 'em."

The outpouring of words choked to a stop in Palmina's throat. She'd never said those things out loud before. She just *did* them. Lived them. Got through them—and helped her gals get through them. That was the most important part. Palmina's own needs became seemingly insignificant in the face of the constant need of these women; in the hardest, most terrible of circumstances where either choice meant a different risk of death for life, different hazards of physical pain and heartbreak.

But now, telling Astryiah these things, suddenly Palmina felt need too. A deep need for the wounds this work had inflicted on her soul to be soothed—to be heard, to be understood, to be forgiven, to be accepted. Simply, to not be alone.

She didn't know how to ask for all that, but Astryiah seemed to know without words what Palmina needed. They were on the too-small bed with the brutally lumpy mattress that had come with this apartment, for Palmina had only one chair in the tiny kitchen that, along with the water closet you could barely turn around in, made up the three "rooms" of her lousy apartment. The only place for two people to sit down together was the back stoop or the bed.

Astryiah sighed, the deep sigh of a woman holding another woman's pain, and folded Palmina into her arms. Palmina had been in those arms plenty of times, dancing, or tripping home from a hop, swacked, in the wee hours of the morning. But this time it was different. It was "all us gals" camaraderie before. Now it was a safe place where she could let go of all she'd been holding on to. It was a *homecoming*.

As her gals had cried in her arms, Palmina let go and cried in Astryiah's arms. Out it all came in sobs and choking gasps. And a startling amount of snot, for which Astryiah silently produced a handkerchief.

At first she was drowning in the immediacy of the pain shaking loose. Then it became a floating in release, safe in warm, strong arms. For a little while, maybe she dozed off; she hadn't been that relaxed in so long. And then with a nasty start, she came to herself, embarrassed for putting her problems on someone else like that. And, equally, for letting anyone see so deeply into her private emotions.

"I...I'm sorry! I been real punchy these days! Please—I'm so sorry—!"

"Hush, *chamuda*, hush. It was a gift you gave to me, your trust. And it was a gift I could give to you, some peace. It is what we *friends* do for each other."

Palmina still felt the hot flush of shame on her skin, despite Astryiah's soothing words, despite her hands softly stroking down Palmina's back. The Vitales were stoic. Well, they were loud enough in anger, and there was no lack of public wailing for the acceptable kinds of loss. But these shameful, private emotions—weaknesses—these were not meant to be shared with *anyone*.

"*Beseder, teraga'.* It is well. Relax. Everyone needs to share their woes and receive comfort now and then. You are not made of stone."

"I don't mean to burden you."

"Be quiet now. I asked for this trust; it is no burden at all." They were silent for a minute, and then she asked, "*Chamuda*, I know I ask much now, but...have you ever needed this...service you provide for women?"

Palmina shuddered, and the tears nearly started again. She'd not let herself even think of that for so, so long. Briefly she fought it. But it rose unstoppably from where she had hidden it down inside.

"Ye-yeah. It's how I found out about it. There was a moment. One of my brother's friends. He said such nice things. We were slap-happy. It felt good. I didn't think that just one time...could lead to...I'd always heard that nothing could happen the first time. Or if he pulled out, and I *did* make him pull out. But in a month, there I was. In that *condition*. And I didn't want to *marry* Jack. He's nice enough, but I don't *love* him—"

Palmina discovered she was talking so fast that she'd forgotten to breathe. She stopped, caught her breath. Astryiah didn't interrupt the silence.

"So. I couldn't have—not right now. I have no money—the factory don't pay much! And I won't—I won't!—move back home. So I couldn't—I just couldn't...!"

"No, *chamuda*, you could not. And I regret that you live in this time and place where you could not have had a safer, healthier experience." Astryiah started to say something else, broke off. She pulled Palmina in, held her tight, as if now she had something *she* was afraid to say. Palmina had never seen Astryiah look the least bit scared of anything.

"Palmina...there is a gift I can give you. It would keep you safe from ever getting pregnant again if you want that freedom. Is that...something you would wish?"

"Not ever getting knocked up, ever? Yeah!"

"Not *ever*."

"Not even if I was married and wanted kids?"

"That is the cost of the gift. You would not be able to be impregnated ever again."

"That's a...real large order."

"It is not an easy decision, no."

"But then...I'd be safe from havin' to go through that all over again?"

"Yes. And you would be...healthier, stronger, safer from disease as well."

"Whatcha talkin' about? A drug? Some kind of operation?"

"No! Nothing like that! Just a...sharing. An intimate sharing."

"That don't jive. Sharing *what?*"

"Ach. This is the hard part. Let me first ask an unspoken question..."

Palmina was going to ask her what she meant, but Astryiah slowly leaned her face closer, and then closer, and then their lips met. Palmina closed her eyes from habit, and without the distraction of vision, she suddenly was not aware of anything except how incredibly soft those lips were, how good they felt against her own. She put all of her surprised self into returning the kiss, and that led to Astryiah wrapping her oddly strong, lithely feminine arms around Palmina and pulling her close for a deeper kiss.

When they finally broke apart, Palmina felt faint. "I never kissed a girl before," she confessed breathlessly to Astryiah.

Her shadow lady smiled. "How did it compare?"

"Oh! You can't compare it! Apples and oranges!"

Astryiah chuckled. "I myself might call it *pomegranates*. Did you like the new fruit?"

"*Yes*. Yes, I did. But—what's that gor to do with keepin' rabbits from dyin'? I mean, obviously you can't knock me up. But you don't just mean *only* makin' whoopee with minnows. I have a feelin' it's real nice, but I don't think it would scratch all my itches."

"No, indeed. And men can certainly be useful for those vexatious itches. What I am offering...is part of the, eh, *process* for making you safe from the negative side effects of scratching that particular itch. It is very hard to describe this process. I do it infrequently, and when I do, I do not need to explain anything...but with you I want to be very clear and candid. I want you to understand and consent—or not, and we go no further.

"My blood has special properties. If I drink blood from you, and you drink from me, that will share those powerful qualities with you. I believe if we do this twice, you will be protected for the rest of your life. For certain, if we did this thrice, you would always be protected...but twice might be enough."

Palmina looked at Astryiah, who looked steadily back, deadly serious. After a few minutes of this, Palmina got up, snagged the grappa bottle, took a deep swig, offered it to

Astryiah. When the latter shook her head, Palmina said, "Right, you don't like this stuff. Not many people do, to be honest."

"It is not that. It is that I drink *only* blood. You have noticed that I eat nothing and drink nothing—you've just been too polite to ask why. I am now telling you why: I am what is called an 'am'r,' and we drink only blood."

"Oh! Like *Dracula* with Bela Lugosi! I loved it! Are you... like that?"

"It was a terrible motion picture. The am'r are nothing like that. Except that, yes, we drink blood."

"I thought Bela Lugosi was a pip!"

"Dracula is nothing like him."

"Dracula is *real?*"

"That is a long story. For another time. We have gotten off the point, which is: I am offering you some of the protection of am'r blood. I am offering you a most intimate gift. It is a complex decision to make."

"Seems like the only decision that matters is if I wanna get in the family way, ever."

"You are not afraid of me drinking your blood? Or of drinking mine?"

"That's all you eat, right?" Astryiah nodded, so Palmina continued, "So I figure it can't be that bad, and you gotta be pretty good at it."

"Oh, *chamuda*, I am very good at it indeed." Astryiah purred this with such assurance that Palmina felt both turned on...but also unnerved. Well, this whole talk was so cockeyed that no wonder she felt unsettled.

"What...what'll it do, besides preventing eating for two?"

"Ah, you will like the other side effects. Your skin and hair will be so fine. You will feel strong, and you will not get sick as easily. I can promise those things, and if you drink only twice, I think they will last you many years until you are old enough that bearing children is no longer a concern."

"You *think?*"

"Well, I have not really, ahhh, experimented. With all who have shared blood with me, we have carried it through to all three times. After that, things are...more certain. But also, ah, there are more consequences."

"What kinda consequences?"

"If we share blood three times, then once you die you will arise back to life, but a life like mine. You will live in the nighttime hours because the sun will be too strong for you. And you will require to feed upon blood as I do. There are many wonderful things, like becoming stronger than mortal humans—we call them "kee"—but those are mere details, which I will tell you about when you want to know more."

Palmina thought for a while. Astryiah let her do so, in her perpetually calm, unbothered manner. Except Palmina thought maybe she was not perfectly serene underneath it. "So, if we only do the blood thing twice, I just get starlet looks and no fella can knock me up? But it might not last? But if we do the blood thing three times, then I become Dracula?"

"Dracula is already Dracula; you would not become him. You would become am'r, like me. Eventually. Also, if we exchange blood three times, well, it would be a bit like getting married. It would be a *commitment.* I do not believe you are ready for this. But I do believe if we share blood only two times, I could give you some protection. I would like to give you that gift."

"Could I, uh, have time to think about this? It's kinda big."

"*B'hechlet.* Certainly. I will return here tomorrow after sunset."

"Uh, later than that. In fact, not tomorrow. I gotta bring a gal to Emma. It might take a while, and maybe she'll sack out here. So, uh, Friday?"

"Very well, *chamuda.* Friday."

"Abyssinia!"

"What? What does the land of Egypt have to do with this?"

"Egypt? Huh? Nah, it's slang. It's 'I'll-be-seein'-ya' all smushed into one word."

"I see. Well then, Abyssinia, dear Palmina, Abyssinia."

Palmina didn't sleep much that night. She could've awfully used the sleep. The next day at the factory dragged interminably, and she could barely force herself to joke around with the gals.

After work, Betty was waiting for her, looking pale but determined. Palmina took her to a diner on the far side of town, following Emma's instructions never to go to her place directly from work or home. Betty couldn't bring herself to eat, but Palmina made her drink a cup of hot coffee with a generous nip of some moonshine she kept in a flask for these purposes.

Emma got the job done, as always. Palmina held Betty's hand through it and held her after as she cried. The cramping and bleeding were bad this time. Betty hadn't figured things out real soon, and it was always so much easier on the girls if they did. The later you left it, the worse it was. But Betty was married and didn't want to spend the night at

Palmina's. "Frank won't like it," she kept saying and insisted on getting up as soon as she could stand. Palmina saw Betty home and gave Frank the excuse that Betty had felt sick at work and gone to rest at her house after, as it was closer to the factory. It was an excuse that had worked with many a husband or father. Mothers could be better—or worse. She waved good night to Betty, who looked haggard enough to support the excuse of feeling poorly.

Palmina got to bed at a decent hour for once.

The next morning at work, all the ladies were whispering. Ethel, who worked beside her on the line, rushed over, pulling on her work smock. "Didja hear 'bout Betty?"

Palmina felt a cold stillness descend over her. "No. What—?"

"She's *dead*. Kicked off in the night. Her man, that Frank, says he has no idea why, that she was right as rain, and then, boom! Gone!"

Linda, on her other side, tutted knowingly. "Betty got herself in a fix. Clear as day."

Palmina made herself reply—didn't know what she said. The gossip moved in a susurration up and down the production line, flowing over her. She did her job automatically, numb to thought or feeling.

Lunch break was a dreaded pause. This was often the time when women who'd gotten themselves in a bad way would sidle up to her and ask about Emma: how to contact her, what the procedure was like, was it really safe? Today nobody came to her for that. Ethel, who was practical and older, unlikely to ever require Emma's services, sat down deliberately beside her.

"So, ya think Betty died from having *it* done?"

Palmina didn't ask how Ethel knew. She wasn't dumb. "I-I dunno. No one's died from it. Not that I know of. Emma's technique's *real* safe. It's from Europe. Actual docs even refer women to her on the Q.T."

"Still. It's a risky thing, something like that. And Betty was never healthy as a horse, was she?"

Palmina thought about how many times Betty had worked through the day hunched over in pain or exhaustion. It was incredible she'd managed to find the time and energy for an affair, given how often she was ill and with Frank demanding his dinner as soon as he got home.

Should she have urged Betty not to get the procedure, knowing that her health wasn't great? But she and Emma had both told Betty the risks. And Betty knew well enough the *other* risks, the complications from pregnancy and birth and the complications of an angry husband. Betty was a grown woman who had made her choices and weighed the stakes. Palmina was not at fault for this death.

But thinking that didn't help her feel any less to blame.

When Astryiah let herself in the back door, as she'd become accustomed to, Palmina raised herself up from where she was crying on her bed with a start. She'd forgotten all about her shadow lady.

"*Chamuda!* What is wrong?"

Astryiah normally hesitated before touching her, Palmina had noticed. A slight, subtle pause before any sort of physical contact. And she never touched anyone else; more than that, Palmina had noticed that strangers, even drunk ones, maintained a respectful distance *from her*. But now Palmina found herself being cradled in those sturdy arms without a second's pause. After the first question, Astryiah asked no more, and Palmina sank into the quiet peacefulness of the other woman.

Not just "woman." An "am'r," whatever that *really* was. Really a vampire, like in the pictures, was it possible?

Astryiah *was* like Dracula, now that she thought about it. Never eating or drinking, arriving only at night, and powerful in the most unexpected ways.

Powerful. And safe. Safe from illness, Astryiah had promised her, and from *pregnancy*.

If she did that blood thing with Astryiah, it would be like Astryiah's arms were around her all the time. She would be protected. And strong. Strong on her own, as Astryiah was, moving through the world as effortlessly as a man, free from the fears and weaknesses of being a *frail*.

In that moment it was all she wanted: strength and freedom. If drinking blood was how she could achieve it, well, she drank grappa, didn't she? Blood couldn't be *worse*. Maybe it was an acquired taste as well. Although she only had to do it two times.

"Astryiah." Her voice was muffled by speaking into a silk-clad shoulder, but the quiet reply was instant.

"Yes, *chamuda?*"

"I'm ready. I wanna do the blood thing."

Astryiah laughed softly. She squeezed Palmina tightly, too tightly for an instant, but just as quickly relaxed, and with a wordless motion in her shoulder, suggested Palmina raise her head.

"I am so glad." Astryiah spoke so low it was almost a whisper. It perfectly captured the intensity of her words.

That was only the start of the intensity. It took quite a while for Astryiah to get to biting Palmina and for Palmina to find out if drinking blood was worse than drinking grappa. Along the way, she found that what she had thought of as "sex" was just a sad approximation of the sensations she could—she *should*—have been feeling. Again and again she was plunged into sensuality beyond anything she had ever expected. By the time Astryiah sank her fangs into Palmina's neck, it held no shock for her, and even the immediate pain got lost in continuing pleasure. By the time Astryiah ripped open her wrist for Palmina to tentatively sip from, she was not truly surprised to discover that that brought its own new, deeper blisses.

Drinking blood left grappa, bathtub gin, moonshine, even that bottle of champagne she once had, in the dust. Even giggle smoke was nothing compared to it.

Afterward, she lay in Astryiah's arms, just as strong as any man's, and luxuriated in how *good* she felt. She had not felt so healthy—so full of joy yet also at peace—in so long she couldn't remember. Perhaps ever since she'd stopped being a kid.

"Is drinking blood always like this?"

"Oh no. Not always. This is a special kind of blood exchange; my people call it "vhoon-vayon." For the am'r, this is the best kind. But as with kee—that's normal people, to you—with kee sex, it is not always this loving or this beautiful."

"You shred it, wheat! Beauteeful is the word! I never felt *anything* like this!" Palmina paused, afraid to say something wrong in the intensity of the bliss that filled her. "Uh, thank you...for all'a this."

"Oh, *chamuda*, it was my pleasure—you cannot know how much pleasure you have given me. But sleep now. You may feel very well indeed, but you need rest after this. And make sure to look in the mirror tomorrow morning. No, I will not tell you why—no more talking! Sleep!"

When Palmina woke up, she could not for a moment remember why she felt so swell. She'd had such a hard day and then a very late night with Astryiah—Oh! She had done *that thing*. And it had not been in any way what she'd expected, and the results were equally nothing like she'd expected. Every movement she made proved this as she bounced off the lumpy old mattress with energy, ease in all her limbs, and a rush of delight in the birdsong outside the window.

Remembering Astryiah's cryptic (even for Astryiah) comment, she rushed to the bathroom. The dark undereye circles that had only been getting darker were gone. Her skin, which had been looking dull from continuous exhaustion, was glowing.

Murder! That blood thing really was *something*.

"You look very well indeed. How have you felt today, *chamuda?*" is what Astryiah said when she came in the back door that evening. She took Palmina's face between her hands and examined her minutely.

"Ring a ding ding! I been aces all day long! Feel like a kid again! All the gals were asking me what new makeup I was using! I can't believe just knocking back a bit of blood could do all that!" Palmina overcame a kind of shyness she'd never had with boys and pushed her face forward through Astryiah's hands to give her a smack on the lips.

Astryiah smiled with such warmth that it transformed her habitually distant expression until she almost seemed a different person. She kissed Palmina back, deep and thorough, a real honey cooler.

"I am pleased that you have taken to it so naturally. But my vhoon, my blood, is not the same as if you had just drunk from any mortal person, any kee. You understand that, *ken?*"

"Uh, guess so. I mean, you've told it to me, but I can't really dig it."

"But you are comfortable with it?"

"Well, I feel real killer-diller! That's comfortable enough!"

"Are you ready to do vhoon-vayon with me again?"

"Have all that fun again? Sure thing!"

"It *is* fun. But it is more than that. This time we will make you so you cannot be impregnated by a man, not ever. I must remind you of this, *chamuda.*"

"That's one of the perks. After what happened to Betty...I don't want that to happen to me, not ever!"

"No, I do not want that either. But I feel I must repeat—must remind you that a child could someday be a thing you wanted as well. My vhoon does not just prevent unwanted pregnancies, but *any* pregnancy..."

Palmina shook her head. "Even when you *want* a baby, if something goes wrong, you'll be pushing up daisies. This sets me free from all that."

"*Lo*, it does. I have seen so many women die from complications in pregnancy, during childbirth, or be crippled by inept delivery. It is a thing undertaken so lightly, but often at such cost. Well, you shall pay another cost then. Come to bed. Let me set you free."

As the blood she'd gulped from Astryiah's wrist made its way into her body, she felt truly freed. For a moment she felt like she had become a bird and she could use brand-new muscles to take off into the air, nothing holding her down ever again.

After she had soared through sensation for a while, suddenly it seemed very silly to her, and she muttered, "Fluttering dickey-birds," one of her favorite swears, and then she was laughing at all of it, and Astryiah was holding her and laughing with her, kissing her with sharp nips of teeth, and she wished the joy of it would never end.

The next morning, she felt as if energy ran through her instead of blood, which would have been a funny ol' thing. Her skin seemed poreless and perfect. Her eyes were bright with health, and the world seemed to sparkle. She sang along with the birds. The night before was still inside her, an echo of euphoria.

It was the weekend. She went shopping for groceries, and on the way stopped in the record store and treated herself to a 45 of Ellington's "Mood Indigo." She should have stopped in to see Babbo and Mamma...but they might have noticed something different about her, and she wasn't ready to answer their questions. She didn't even know how to answer her own questions, the ones that bubbled in the back of her mind, waiting to be considered when the exhilaration wore off.

She was starving; she couldn't get enough food to eat. She made up a huge batch of pasta fazool, which normally she'd share with friends whom she felt didn't get enough hot meals. Today she ate almost the whole pot, one bowl after another. She didn't get indigestion, but did eventually find relief from the intense hunger.

There was a hop that night, and she dragged Astryiah to it, and they danced to every song. Palmina felt the same endless energy moving through her that she'd seen in Astryiah. The hot jazz pumped through her like an external, communal heart.

As Astryiah saw her home, with the sky softening to a lighter purply-blue where the sun was going to rise, she was still feeling the rhythms moving her muscles, and she took Astryiah's hand and spun them along the empty street. Astryiah laughed with her and didn't let go of her hand.

"Why didn't ya share your, uh, vhoon, with me before this? I coulda been feelin' this sweet all this time!"

"I am so very pleased you are happy with your choice, *chamuda*. But it is a very intimate and intense thing. It is a risk I take, to reveal that aspect of myself to you. Many kee could not handle such information. They would want to kill me for being a monster. As in your *Dracula* film."

"Risk? But *you're* not scared of anything! And you're nothing like Dracula! This, what I feel, this is nothing like that. You're not a monster. You—you're a lifesaver! I feel so full of life. *Dracula* was all about *death*."

Astryiah stopped. She took Palmina's other hand and looked down at her, more seriously than Palmina had ever seen that solemn face. "I'm afraid I have failed to convey to you what gift you have accepted from me." She looked around and led Palmina to a small park between buildings, just a few benches and some grass and trees. With no streetlight, the shadows made it a space of enveloping privacy. Palmina realized she'd normally never have felt safe in an unlit part of the city, until she'd walked at night with Astryiah.

Astryiah sat them down on a bench and started speaking with low urgency. "*Chamuda*, I do not know if you are just giddy with my vhoon—it does take some kee like that—but I fear that your lack of understanding may bring you pain or worse hurt.

"I bring death, like your Dracula. That is what you said you wanted. With only two sharings of blood, I have rendered your body unable to bring forth life in the normal, kee way. This strength you feel rushing through you is not the strength of life, not in the way you know, but a strength that doesn't meet its full potential until your own kee death. You have drunk of death, *neshama sheli*—my soul, and I have not saved you. You are right that there is strength from *sheol*, and we may harness it to make our time in this world, however long, a more loving and powerful life.

"By going only this far with me, I think I prevent you from finding the disadvantages of my existence; you get only a small taste of the advantages. But do not doubt that the changes you feel within you are from brushing too close to death, not from some bright flame of life."

In the deep shadow of the park, Palmina could not see Astryiah's face, not well. She could see the outline of her head and a little light catching on nose and cheek, a low gleam from the shiny honey-colored marcel waves, perfectly styled as always. Palmina wondered if she could see a little better in the dark than before, but it wasn't enough to read her dusky dame's face; only the tone of voice and the pressing of Astryiah's urgent fingers against hers gave her the true impression of how serious this was.

"You're right; I don't dig it, not all the way. I know I feel just *aces*. I know how safe I feel around you and how safe I feel with your vhoon inside me now. But how can I *really* understand it? I don't hardly know *anything* about you, about your life. I don't even know why you're here in Philly. You could be anywhere in the world. Whatcha doin' *here?*"

"I am here with you. For now, I am your lover and protector."

Palmina shook her head in frustration. "No—what for didja come here, before you met me?"

"I was traveling around the States. It is a very young place with many problems, but in some ways reminds me of my home—a very old place, but with problems which are ever renewing."

"OK, but what for were ya in the alley behind my place that first night?"

"Ehhhh. Well." Astryiah paused. A long pause. Palmina bit her tongue to keep from asking any other questions, thereby giving Astryiah a way out of answering.

"Well, I had heard of Emma. And that you were the best connection to her. I found you first."

Palmina's head spun.

"What could *you* 've possibly wanted from Emma? *You* can't get in that kinda trouble."

"Ehhhh. *Lo.* Well, in a different way than I have helped you, I could help Emma, and you, and all of Emma's clients."

"'Help'." Palmina's voice was flat.

"*Ken, ken!*" Astryiah sounded almost-nervous for the second time Palmina had ever heard. "I could be of great help! But then I met you, and I did not know how to make the offer without perhaps causing offense. And then...I did not want to risk offense even further and losing you from my life. This time with you...has been a rare delight for me."

Palmina pushed the compliment away with a wave of her hand. "How do you think you can *help?*"

"Ehhhh. Well...if I drink from a woman who is pregnant and who does not want to be, and if I give her just one small mouthful of my vhoon, her body will abort. It is much safer for the women, even than Emma's modern methods. I wanted to offer that medically safer option."

"But. You didn't. You just did a different thing with me."

"Well, I developed feelings for you, a connection with you. It made it harder."

"Harder to help other women?"

"*Lo...!* Just. Clouded. Complicated."

Palmina felt a surge of anger, brighter than any anger she'd felt before. Everything was so much more intense now. She fought to keep her voice level; even in this rush of emotion, she could tell that Astryiah wouldn't put up with any beef.

"Please. Square up why your plans changed when ya met me."

"I cannot explain. Please accept this. It is about emotion, and it is hard for me to talk about. I believe I have made it quite plain how I feel about you. I was...concerned that I might...scare you away...if I made my original offer to you, once our friendship had begun."

Palmina pushed down the cascade of emotions that threatened to come out at top volume. Her family dealt with emotions loudly and at length. She was comfortable with that. She *really* wanted to blow her wig right now. But—and here was a voice inside her that she tried to ignore—while being around Astryiah made her feel safe from others, a part of her was intensely aware that Astryiah was dangerous like a gun, like fire: something that *could* protect you but wasn't guaranteed to be something that *wouldn't* hurt you. Kill you, even.

"Well. Now I know. So what's this offer, exactly?"

Astryiah could not miss the lack of emotion in her voice or the way she held herself so still and distant. She felt Astryiah's body echo hers, pulling away from her on the bench. She almost reached out after her, but then she heard Astryiah's voice, so cold it hurt to hear, replying, "It is a simple offer. Instead of bringing the women who need help to Emma for the procedure she uses, they could be brought to a nice warm hotel room where I would be. Or someone's back bedroom. Not the dangerous spaces you have found for the procedure. They would be given just enough information to consent: that they would lose some blood and drink a small amount of 'medicine,' and then they would not have any danger, just a heavy period, some cramping. I am very far from being in a kee body, so I do not remember anymore what all is involved, only that it would never cause injury and never create a situation like poor Betty. They would just need a good hot meal, and then they could go back to their lives unharmed. Well, except for what emotions they must endure from the loss."

Palmina thought for a long while. Astryiah waited like a statue.

"I'm not sure I'd'a believed you or what you'd've had to *do* to get me to believe you if you'd talked to me about alla this that first night. I think I dig why you did whatcha did... but I still don't *like* it. Makes me feel like you were using me."

"This is unfortunate. I was trying to keep you from assuming I was only interested in you for vhoon; *that* is why I changed my plans."

They sat in the silent shadows, neither sure where to go from there.

"Maybe you oughta—" Palmina started as Astryiah began, "Perhaps I had best—" Both came to a screeching verbal halt. Astryiah eventually finished her sentence. "Perhaps I had best go away for a while to give you time to think."

She didn't want that, but she made herself say, "Yeah... maybe you better."

And then she was alone in the dark.

When Astryiah left, she took joy with her, more joy than Palmina had realized was in her life. She'd been so exhausted and worn down for so long she hadn't realized how Astryiah's wry observances of life had bolstered her up. Even before the vhoon-vayon, she'd come to count on that fixed presence in her nights, the intimacy in words long before intimacy of bodies.

Words, words spoken in the dark where they could safely be said.

Bodies, bodies intertwining in the dark where fingers and teeth could break through barriers which would have been too impermeable in daylight.

As soon as Astryiah had left the painful void in her wake, Palmina was able to entirely understand and excuse her actions. Once it was too late to take back her words.

Maybe she'll come back? She said, "Go away for a while." That means she'll come back someday,

Life went on. At least it did for everyone else. At the factory, the biscuits went along the production line, as did the intrigues and gossip. Palmina smiled, but it did not touch her; it did not feel as *real* as anything Astryiah had brought into her life. At the dances, the jazz was hot, but the music did not touch her pulse. The girls would say she'd "run out of gas," and it sure felt like that, all right.

As life went on, the problems of life continued as well. It was not a week after Astryiah had left only terrible emptiness in her wake that a gal whispered to her at the end of the lunch break, "I need to see Emma. *Please.*"

The weeks went by. Another lady needed Emma's services. Each was sick afterward. Nobody shared Betty's fate. But as she escorted the shaken women to their homes, eyes red and skin drained of color, she thought about how much easier and safer it *could* have been for them. *I denied them that. My high-hat made it harder for 'em.*

Guilt was the only thing that she felt acutely through the numb ache of loss and regret. The rest of her existence seemed far away, the sound muted, her senses dulled.

Her vhoon-boosted health was so robust that she shouldn't have been able to feel down. She got compliments—and demands for her beauty secrets—every day. Men flocked to her, and it took everything she'd learned from Astryiah to fend them off. It seemed she would not need Astryiah's exotic birth control; she felt no desire to put up with fumbling hands on her body when she remembered her shadow woman's skillful, intuitive fingers. She had no urge to play the flirtation game with anyone less coolly ironic or excitingly worldly.

She tried not to think about how the other women could have benefited from Astryiah's powerful blood, even as she connected them to Emma and took them to and from their procedures.

She didn't go to the New Year's hop or any parties her friends were having. She went to bed early and the next day cooked several batches of spaghetti so she could give out dishes of it to various friends who were down on their luck. Her appetite had gone back to normal over the months, so cooking for others was doable again. Since it was a day off from work, she distracted herself by cooking and delivering bowls wrapped in towels to keep them warm.

With the remaining sauce simmering and the simmering water just poured off the last batch of pasta, the tiny kitchen had become too hot, so she went out to sit on the back stoop for a minute. She'd cool down real quick in a Philly January.

"Have you perhaps any grappa to share?" The voice had been too longed-for, too anxiously anticipated, for her to recognize it at first. Her head came up sharply, and there in the twilight's purple gloom was her lady of the shadows.

"Nah. I didn't feel like getting sauced alone today." Her months-long blues helped her to answer coolly instead of running up and throwing her arms around Astryiah. Getting her hopes up seemed too hard, even with the woman she'd pined for standing right there in front of her.

"I could keep you company," Astryiah offered. It was the only vulnerability she would show, Palmina knew; this one advance, this one risk of rejection. And if it was turned down, Astryiah would disappear out of her life forever.

"There's room here for you to sit," she answered carefully. She was afraid. Afraid to say something wrong: to try too hard or be perceived to not be trying hard enough. Astryiah could be spooked so easily, and she felt no confidence that she could stop or repair it.

"Well," Astryiah said when she had settled down beside Palmina. Their thighs had a hairbreadth of space carefully held between them. "You needed time to think. Have I given you long enough to consider everything?"

"Yes! Yes. You did. I have." Palmina found it hard, in the moment, to say things she'd so desperately wished she could have said before. "Look—I'm sorry."

"You need not apologize. The am'r world is different from the one you are used to. Different principles. Different purposes. Different focuses and importances. You are not of that world, so things I say can shock your sensibilities. I am long since departed from your kee worldview. I pushed you too far, too fast."

"You gave me time! I know you tried to tell me. I just couldn't hear it, not right away. But I dig it now. I do. I promise."

"You are really come to an understanding?" Astryiah did not look hopeful, just serious.

"I am! I wantcha'ta help as many women as possible. I wanna *help* you help as many women as possible."

Astryiah paused and looked dead in Palmina's eyes. "I must clearly ask you now. I must know that you do truly accept all that that means. I will drink the blood of those women, giving them a small portion of mine in return."

"Yeah, yeah. That jives."

"And you and I...*we* cannot do vhoon-vayon again. Not unless you choose to leave your kee life and enter my am'r one, leaving your friends and family behind."

"I...understand. At least, I *believe* ya, since I can't really understand."

"*Tov!* We will work together to help these women. I am very glad you want this. Very glad, *chamuda*."

"Can we...uh...can we, just, you know, *cuddle?* Be in bed, without the blood?"

Astryiah got a complicated but not unhappy look on her face. "I do not normally 'be in bed' with one with whom I am not vhoon-sharing. However...I have missed how you feel in my arms, dear Palmina. You are exceptional, so I will make an exception for you."

Palmina found herself in Astryiah's arms, smelling the slightly musky-seawater-metallic scent of her, feeling the firmly muscled body melt around her to fit together best.

If anyone had been keeping track of such things, they would have noticed that for about a decade, few women in Philadelphia and its immediate environs died of certain "unexplained causes," and fewer unplanned babies were thrust into an unwelcoming world.

"Nothing lasts forever—at least not the good stuff," Palmina would reflect later, in the community for the elderly where she'd found a comfy little cottage she could maintain by herself as the aches and pains of age slowed her down. "But for a while we did some good, we did."

She said as much to the woman who held her in her arms on the final day. She had given up eating a week ago; a graceful exit from a graceless disease like cancer. When life lost its joys, it was time to go, and she was at peace. Her friends had visited her bedside to say goodbye. She was ready, and the pain was bad enough that she was more than ready.

She told them all to leave for the night—no sense in anyone sleeping in a chair, waiting around for death with her. She could go to sleep in peace—and better if she didn't wake up in the morning to have yet another "final day."

But she did wake up, in the middle of the night. To find familiar arms around her, so familiar that for a confused moment she didn't know which decade it was. "Ah—Astryiah?"

"Shhh, *chamuda*. I am here, here for the last night, here to take away the final pain. I missed how you felt in my arms, and I could not let you go without feeling that one more time."

Palmina laughed with delight. "I'm like a bag of sticks now! I sure don't feel like I usta!"

"You still feel like my dear Palmina."

"I'm so glad you're here. You were the only one I couldn't say goodbye to. Didn't wanna go without that—although I never expected to get the chance."

"But here I am, *chamuda*. Feel my arms around you. Let me help you say goodbye."

"Abyssinia…"

"*Ken, ken*, I remember. We said this back then, didn't we? Abyssinia, Palmina, my love. Abyssinia."

Note on Abyssinia

Astryiah is another of the am'r who has been a side character all through the Blood & Ancient Scrolls series, and who is always going to demand that I give her more screen time, as it were.

Astryiah is not even her given name, and she's never told me what it was. In the *Sefer Hasidim* there is a story of an ancient vampire of that name, who uses her hair to strangle her victims. So that makes Astryiah one of the "known in the kee world" am'r, along with Dracula (now going by "Sandu," of course), The Black Vampyre in *Teeth are Bones*, and the biggest Big Bad, The Vampire of Croglin Grange in *Blood Ad Infinitum*. Most am'r managed to fly under kee radar, but Astryiah is too intense and has lived too long to have stayed completely invisible.

This story is based on the life of my Grandma. She actually lived in Philly at that time-period, and the surface details of her life are similar. She helped women to access the services of a local abortionist. She never spoke about that part of her life directly to me, but after her death I've gotten detailed notes from my mother, and confirmation from another source. Obviously, the part about sharing blood with an am'r is unlikely to be true, but then again...we will never know for sure!

A fun aspect of this story is that it's in the third person. I adore writing in the third person, but Noosh's story (which is how this whole series started) felt like it had to be first person...and sometimes I've regretted that, since, as I'm stuck in first person for the rest of the series. But at least in short stories and novellas I get to play in a different point of view, which is a real relief.

This story obviously still takes place in the world of the Blood & Ancient Scrolls Series, but it's set long before Noosh or any of the modern characters were even a twinkle in anyone's eyes. I hope you enjoy this blast to the past, and a non-Noosh view of the am'r!

Thank you to my Grandma, for all the work you did in you life to make the world a better place, and for inspiring me in the kitchen, at the sewing machine, for this story, and *every day* to try and live up to your example. I miss you daily, and would give anything to sit down with you over a plate of your amazing spaghetti and hear the story about the cat and the Locatelli again!

INDEX OF NON-ENGLISH PHRASES

PHRASE • TRANSLATION • LANGUAGE

Ale! • Go! • Kreyòl

Aye, yer an awfy blether, ya bampot. • Yes, you talk too much, you fool. • Scottish

Ayisyen • Haitian • Kreyòl

Ayiti • Haiti • Kreyòl

b'hechlet • certainly • Hebrew

baton-lamnò • baton of death • Kreyòl

bawbag • the scrotum; also an ignorant, obnoxious, or otherwise debatable person • Scottish slang

Beseder, teraga'. • It is well, relax. • Hebrew

Bíddu! • Wait! • Norse

blan • white • Kreyòl

bon • good • Kreyòl

Bonswa! • Hello, good evening! • Kreyòl

bróðir minn • my brother • Old Norse

Bwa Kayiman • Alligator Forest • Kreyòl

Certo! • Certainly! • Italian

chamuda • cutie, sweetie • Hebrew

chen sal • dirty dog • Kreyòl

cheri • dear • Kreyòl

chouchou • "cabbage-cabbage," darling • Kreyòl

clusterbùrach • mix of modern clusterfuck and bùrach, mess • Scottish slang

corvée • a form of unpaid forced labor • Kreyòl

Crìosdaidheachd • Christianity • Scottish Gaelic

Dan konn mòde lang. • Teeth are known to bite the tongue. • Kreyòl

De kòk kalite pa rete nan menm baskou. • Two good cocks do not stay in the same farmyard. • Kreyòl

Delivrans • Deliverance (name) • Kreyòl

désocupation • de-occupation • Kreyòl

dunderclunk • A big, stupid person • Scottish slang

eejit • idiot • Scottish slang

enbesil • imbecile • Kreyòl

euskaldunak • Basque word for themselves • Basque

faol-chù, mo • wolf, my • Scottish Gaelic

fífl • fool, idiot • Old Norse

fout maren • fucking Marine • Kreyòl

fout sal • fucking filthy • Kreyòl

Frøken • dated term for "Miss" • Norse/Norwegian

Hjartabroti • Heartbreaker • Old Norse

gason (ti) • boy (little) • Kreyòl

Gendarmerie d'Haïti • Haiti's only military force from 1916-1928 • Kreyòl

Je wè bouch pe. • The eyes see, the mouth is shut. • Kreyòl

ken • yes • Hebrew

Kite'l ale! • Let him go! • Kreyòl

kolaboratris • collaborator (f) • Kreyòl

køuærne • little dog • Scottish Gaelic

Lang pa lanmè, men li ka neye-w. • The tongue is not the sea, but it can drown you. • Kreyòl

li santi fò • he stunk badly • Kreyòl

litilmenni • one of little manhood (n) • Old Norse

lo • no • Hebrew

Lwa • spirits of Vodou • Kreyòl

Madanm • madam, ma'am • Kreyòl

manbo • priestess • Kreyòl

maren Ameriken • American Marine • Kreyòl

Men wi non! • "But yes no!" is an emphatic "No!" • Kreyòl

merde • shit • Kreyòl

mèsi • thank you • Kreyòl

miklimunnr • big mouth / loud mouth • Old Norse

miri-cath • battle-madness • Scottish Gaelic

Mjǫtuðr • "dispenser of fate" • Old Norse

mo bhràthair • my brother • Scottish Gaelic

Montagnes Noires • Black Mountains • Kreyòl

muckle • big, huge, great • Scottish

Na sniggering fae ye, arsepiece! • No laughing from you, asshole! • Scottish slang

nèg • person • Kreyòl

nei • no • Old Norse

neshama sheli • my soul • Hebrew

Naw, naw, dinnae tak' it lik' that! • No, no, don't take it like that! • Scottish slang

Non, non, pa enkyete. • No, no, don't worry. • Kreyòl

okipan Ameriken • American occupation • Kreyòl

Ou se lanmou kè mwen. • You are the love of my heart. • Kreyòl

Ou! Se yon ravet fout sal ou ye! • You! You're a fucking filthy cockroach! • Kreyòl

Pa gen bon rezon. • No good reason. • Kreyòl

pitit tig se tig • a tiger's cub is a tiger • Kreyòl

plaçage • a traditional recognized extralegal civil union • Kreyòl

pointeach • pointy • Scottish Gaelic

Poukisa? • Why? • Kreyòl

Premye so pa so. • A missed first try does not count. • Kreyòl

radge wee shite • crazy little shit • Scottish slang

richt enuff • right enough • Scottish slang

revolisyon ayisyen • Haitian Revolution • Kreyòl

Sa ki pa touye ou, li angrese ou. • What does not kill you, fattens you. • Kreyòl

schiltron/skjaldborg • shield wall • Scottish Gaelic/Old Norse

se vre • it's true • Kreyòl

sètènman • certainly • Kreyòl

sheol • the underworld place of stillness and darkness which awaits after death • Hebrew

Shut yer puss, ya lavvy-heided wankstain. • Shut your mouth, you toilet-headed cumsplat. • Scottish slang

Siùrsach • Bitch • Scottish Gaelic

skeggøx • bearded-axe • Old Norse

Souke tèt pa kase kou. • You can shake your head, but do not break your neck. • Kreyòl

Tire Machèt • Hatian martial art • Kreyòl

Tov! • Good! • Hebrew

Use Sans Moindre Contrôle • 'Has No Self Control' (nickname for the U.S. Marine Corps) • Kreyòl

vakabon • hoodlum • Kreyòl

veslingr • puny wretch • Old Norse

Víkingr/Víkingar • Viking/Vikings • Old Norse

vinurinn • friend, "mate" • Old Norse

Whit did ah say? Ye'r a muckle gowk, na doubt! • What did I say? You're a big fool, for sure! • Scottish slang

wi • yes • Kreyòl

yanki • Yankee • Kreyòl

yer richt • you're right • Scottish

yfir-berserkr • uber-berserker • Old Norse

Yon jou pou chasè, yon jou pou jibye. • The hunter has his day, but the prey has his day as well. • Kreyòl

winching • "wenching," going out in pursuit of active female companionship • Scottish slang

zanmi mwen • my friend • Kreyòl

Glossary of the Am'r Language

AM'R WORD • DEFINITION

adharmhem • one who endangers the am'r as a whole, or the act of endangering the am'r as a whole

ahstha • coma am'r fall into when deprived of enough blood and/or oxygen

am'r (sing. & pl.) • commonly known as a "vampire" or "strigoi mort"

am'r-nafsh (sing. & pl.) • In Romanian, a "strigoi viu." A living human being who shared blood with an am'r three times, but not yet died.

Aojasc' am'ratv! • "Strength and immortality!"

aojysht (sing), **aojyshtaish** (pl.) • am'r elder

bakheb-vhoonho • giver of blood, used for am'r who give blood to other am'r or kee. This is a term used for the stronger blood going to the weaker, whether am'r or kee

cinyaa • my lover

esteshcinast • verb: to know by smell, specifically to recognize the vhoon-anghyaa of other am'r *(present tense: "I esteshcinasti", past tense "I have esteshcinastii")*

fraheshteshnesh • first blood meal as a newly awoken am'r

frangkhilaat • to feed/take nutrition from a kee

frithaputhra (sing.), **-ish** (pl.) • "beloved child," title used by an am'r for an am'r / am'r-nafsh made with the former's blood

gharpatar • grandfather, maker of my maker

izchha (sing.), **-ish** (pl.) • a "sacrifice," a mortal who is selected to donate blood (with or without sex)

kee (sing. & pl.) • mortal, non-vampire, living human being

maadak • intoxicating drink; poison, gets kee high, effects am'r like strong hallucinogen / tranquilizer

maadakyo • corrupted with maadak, a mortal who has drunk maadak

pat'rkosh • patar-killer

patar • "parent" or "maker"; title used by an am'r or am'r-nafsh for the am'r who made them

tokhmarenc • finishing another vampire, dying the final death

vhoon • blood

vhoon-anghyaa • blood influence, blood-line, the traits that come down from your patar, also the smell of your patar in your blood

vhoon-berefteh • to be bled

vhoon-vaa • am'r-style healing with blood

vhoon-vayon • am'r love making, with other am'r or am'r-nfash

vistarascha • dying the mortal death, becoming am'r

The Blood & Ancient Scrolls Series

I f you enjoyed these tales, there's so much more to explore in the world of the Blood & Ancient Scrolls series! Get FREE stories by signing up for Raven's Newsletter

Please request them to be carried by your local library or bookshop.

Go to https://ravenbelas.co/to snag signed paperbacks from the author!

Or buy them at your preferred online vendor:

Book I *Blood Ex Libris*: https://books2read.com/bxl

Book II *Blood Sine Qua Non*: https://books2read.com/bsqn

Book III *Blood Ad Infinitum*: https://books2read.com/bai

About Raven Belasco

Raven Belasco has been fascinated by vampires since she was 12 years old. You probably shouldn't let 12-year-olds read Stoker's Dracula, but Raven grew up in a house where, if she could get the book off the shelf, she could read it. Raven also grew up with her backyard mostly comprised of a cemetery filled with graves ranging from the late 1600s through 1800s. If spending your childhood playing on old graves doesn't prepare you for a career writing about the (un)dead, then probably nothing will.

Raven has been writing for magazines and in the publishing field since her twenties. She currently devotes her time to the demands of the am'r, to building Immoral Influence Publications, and to training a terrier to be a Good Boy—none of which are small endeavours!

To keep up with the Blood & Ancient Scrolls series, you can sign up for Raven's Newsletter at https://ancientscroll s.beehiiv.com/subscribe

Or find her online: https://ravenbelas.co/

Immoral Influence Publications

"All influence is immoral" — *Oscar Wilde*

Immoral Influence Publications is built on rejection of toxic traditional publishing practices, with a respect and embrace of the beneficial ones.

IIP is all about the "slow food" mentality. We are here to nurture writers who don't fit into the "publish as often as you can churn the books out" indie book mentality. We are authors who care about well-researched, beautifully crafted tales, well-edited and reviewed with sensitivity, laid out with loving care in attractive books.

IIP is 1000% about diverse characters and fresh voices.

We are starting small, building slowly, with a dedication to quality and originality from the very foundation. You can expect excellence from all our works, but also a twinkle of mischief and a sincere desire to break boundaries in genre and take everything to the next level.

Visit us at immoralinfluence.com